HIS FIRST WIFE

HIS FIRST WIFE
A PSYCHOLOGICAL THRILLER

JACK DANE

To the Psychological Thriller Readers Facebook Group. Thank you endlessly for your continued support of my author career. I truly couldn't do it without your help. This one is for all of you-if you read this, shoot me a message for a virtual high-five :)

CONTENTS

Prologue	1
1. ABBY	3
2. Abby	11
3. Spencer	17
4. Abby	22
5. Abby	28
6. Spencer	34
7. Abby	40
8. Abby	48
9. Shannon	54
10. Abby	61
11. Abby	68
12. Abby	75
13. Abby	80
14. Abby	84
15. Spencer	94
16. Shannon	97
17. Abby	101
18. Abby	104
19. Abby	109
20. Shannon	114
21. Abby	119
22. Spencer	126
23. Abby	130
24. Abby	140
25. Abby	145
26. Abby	151
27. Abby	159
28. Spencer	164
29. Abby	172
30. Abby	177
31. Spencer	183
32. Shannon	191
33. Abby	195
34. Spencer	201
Epilogue	206

Also by Jack Dane 211
About the Author 213

ABOUT HIS FIRST WIFE

He's the perfect husband...if you can forget the rumors about his first wife.

Abby is happily married to her dream guy–handsome, hardworking, and completely devoted.

Sure, there are those nagging rumors about the **mysterious disappearance of his first wife**, but Abby trusts the man she married.

Until an unmarked letter arrives and upends her life in a single sentence.

YOU DON'T KNOW YOUR HUSBAND.

She has to find out what the letter means. After all, if there's one person you truly know, it's the person you've married...right?

But the more Abby finds out, the more terrified she becomes. As dark secrets come to light, she realizes that uncovering the truth **might be the last thing she ever does**.

Fans of Freida McFadden, Daniel Hurst, and Kiersten Modglin will love this fast-paced psychological thriller that will leave you guessing until the crazy, twisted end.

PROLOGUE

SHANNON

SEVEN YEARS AGO

There isn't much time.

He'll be home soon.

I take a final glance around the bedroom. Our bedroom.

How happy I once was here. Young and in love. Those memories exist now only in the framed pictures lining the dresser.

Shaking myself, I zip up my duffel bag. There isn't much at all in it, but I don't care. It'll have to be enough. I just need to get away—while I still can.

The car is packed for our trip, ready and waiting for my husband to come home.

When he does, he'll find me already gone. I don't know what will happen after that, but I don't care anymore.

All that matters is getting away.

I take a final glance around the room before heaving the duffel bag strap up onto my shoulder and stepping through the doorway.

The living room is quiet, with only a couple of lamps illuminating the space.

More pictures. More memories. Good riddance.

The journey down to the parking garage takes longer than I want. It seems like the elevator stops on every floor, people stepping on and off.

Seemingly every resident in the building has somewhere to go today. Never before have I been jealous of those living in first-floor apartments.

Each time the door opens, I imagine him standing there on the other side, his chin lifting, those bright blue eyes coming up to pin me against the wall.

I make it to the parking garage and look for our car. I wouldn't even have come down here, save for the fact that he packed both our passports. Something tells me that was on purpose.

The car's parked around the corner.

I hurry across the cement floor, my footsteps sounding extra loud to my ears as they echo through the cavernous space.

As I go, I pull out the braid in my hair, just to give my anxious hands something to focus on.

I'm alone down here, as far as I can tell. Even still, my pulse has reached jackhammer levels. I have to be quick about this.

Get the passport, get out.

When I round the corner, however, I stop walking.

There's our car—and right beside it, the suitcase.

Only the last time I saw it, it was in the trunk. My heart pounds against my ribs. How did—

A scrape from behind me. I jerk around.

It turns out I'm not alone in the parking garage after all.

CHAPTER 1
ABBY

I know everyone says it, but I truly am the luckiest girl in the world.

I live in a beautiful apartment in New York City, just a few blocks from Central Park.

I married the man of my dreams, just as I knew I would.

Turning over in bed, I let out a yawn as my eyes fall across Spencer's peaceful sleeping form beside me.

He's always so calm in his sleep, reminding me of a Disney prince or something. I know it sounds a little creepy, but sometimes I just like to watch him and marvel at how I got so lucky.

Seems like these days, every man is doing something wrong.

Many of the friends I grew up with back home are divorced now after having thought they'd found their forever person.

Me on the other hand—I can only offer my condolences and be grateful for how lucky I am. I really have found the perfect man.

Spencer is kind and loving. He's charming and handsome

and has a high-paying job he works hard at. Truly, the perfect man.

Sometimes that job means he's gone for days at a time on work trips, but I know he would never do anything to break my trust.

A shrill beeping sounds from the other side of the bed. Spencer's phone snapping him awake with his daily alarm.

He works in private equity, a lucrative career that has provided us quite the life in New York City.

At thirty years old, it's pretty rare to be able to afford such a nice apartment in Tribeca.

Of course I never could have moved in here on my own, but with our combined incomes, we were able to pull it off.

Spencer sits up in the bed with a slight grunt, looking around wildly for a moment before his eyes settle on me. He breaks into a smile. His voice is pleasantly rough with sleep.

"Good morning."

"Good morning," I reply.

I love the way he looks at me every morning, as if seeing me for the first time. It's one of the reasons I fell in love with him.

No man has ever looked at me the way he does. Even better, Spencer tells me that he's never loved a woman the way he loves me.

That's refreshing to hear from a guy, especially considering my track record.

Somehow in past relationships, I always seemed to be the one who loved the hardest, which meant I hurt the most when those breakups came.

Not with Spencer.

I'm not his first wife though.

If there *was* anything wrong with Spencer, and really it's only a little thing, it's that he's been married once before.

He doesn't talk about it often, and I can understand why.

Apparently, people still pester him about it, which makes me feel so sorry for him. Sometimes I wish I could scream from the rooftops that he was cleared by the police of any wrongdoing.

He's innocent, and after nearly five years of marriage, he's proven to me that I'm the only woman that truly matters to him.

We begin our morning routine as usual, Spencer slipping off to the bathroom to take a shower as I step into the kitchen and start getting the coffee ready to go. We work well as a team.

I throw some eggs into the skillet, turning them so they don't burn as I hear the shower switch on from behind the closed bathroom door.

Spencer is humming some song he's had stuck in his head for the past couple of days, but it doesn't bother me.

Out of all the potential things that could be going wrong between a married couple, I'll settle for the biggest irritation being a repetitive song.

After the eggs are cooked, I get some bacon going. The smell of the burning sugar has my stomach rumbling within seconds.

As the bacon sizzles on the pan, I reach over and grab a couple of plates out of the cabinet to put them on the island side-by-side. We always eat breakfast together.

It's our little just-us time before the day gets hectic, and we each have our attention pulled toward other things.

As usual, I won't see him until much later tonight, long after the sun has gone down, so it's important to cherish this special morning connection time.

Spencer emerges from the bathroom with a towel wrapped around his waist, dark hair slicked back from his face and his skin a little pink.

He heads over to the bedroom closet to pick out a suit for the day.

I study his bare back through the open doorway, admiring his physique, grateful for how hard he works to stay in shape.

His hair is curling a little as it dries, the thick layers tempting me to run my hands through them.

As if Spencer could be any more perfect, he flashes me another smile in the mirror while buttoning his white dress shirt.

As always, that smile makes my belly a little fluttery.

"What?" he asks as his grin widens.

I shake my head.

"Nothing," I reply, but now I'm smiling too.

I'm just so happy. I truly don't know how I got this lucky.

Once he has his pants and shoes on, Spencer throws his suit jacket over his shoulder and emerges from the bedroom to join me at the kitchen island. He lets out a small groan as he slips onto one of the barstools.

"Abby, you spoil me," he announces before going to town on his breakfast.

A sensation of warmth fills my chest at his compliment. I like spoiling him.

"What've you got going on today?" he asks.

"Not much, just work and seeing Katherine for a walk," I reply.

Spencer nods as he chews. "You know, I still haven't met her. You've got to get her over to the apartment some time so I can finally meet your best friend."

I giggle and poke him playfully as I reach for the TV remote.

"If you didn't work so much, it'd be a lot easier to schedule something."

How wonderful he wants to meet my friends. As my eyes digest the words on the television however, the warm feeling inside me fades away.

WOMAN FOUND MURDERED IN CENTRAL PARK, reads the byline across the bottom of the television.

I shake my head, my stomach twisting as they flash pictures of the victim up on the screen. She looks so young.

Her poor family. Then my thoughts turn to my own family.

I hope my mom doesn't get wind of this on the national news. This is exactly what she thinks happens to girls who move from small town Iowa to New York City.

Of course there are about four million of us in the city, and the vast majority are perfectly safe, but it does happen, and when it does, it naturally sends a chill through the rest of us.

When I see things like this on the news, I can't blame my mom for worrying.

My voice catches in my throat as I try to speak, and I have to swallow before getting the words out.

"How horrible."

I glance over to see Spencer's reaction, but he's looking at his phone and not paying attention.

"Honey," I say.

This time he looks up, but only for a moment. "Yeah, how sad."

Spencer burps and then pockets his phone. "I've got to get going. Movie tonight?"

We've made a habit of watching a movie almost every night. That might seem excessive to some people, but we both love movies, and it's become our routine.

We discuss the options for tonight briefly and settle on some cheesy horror movie that'll have me snuggling close to Spencer and clutching him through the jump scares.

With breakfast finished, he sucks down the rest of his coffee then plants a kiss on my lips as he readies himself to head out the door.

"I love you," I say, moving in close for one more goodbye kiss before I let him go.

"I love you, too," he says, his eyes finding mine and holding the connection a second.

I feel my cheeks flush as they do every time he says that.

The embrace lasts another moment before Spencer tosses a glance at his phone and sees the time.

He lets out a curse before chuckling and heading toward the door.

"The value won't be provided for the shareholders by itself," he quips as he pulls open the door.

He turns around and gives me one last wave, blowing me a kiss before pulling the door shut.

I can hear his footsteps heading down the hall for just another moment before Spencer is totally gone.

Settling back into my seat, I take another sip of my coffee. Time to ready myself for another day.

I work remotely, which has its advantages and disadvantages.

On the one hand, I don't have to worry about getting all dolled up and facing the subway system every morning like Spencer does.

I do have work hours, but I can do the job wherever I like, which is nice.

On the other hand, I sometimes feel like this lifestyle can be a little isolating.

Sure, I have Spencer—whom I'm immensely grateful for—and Katherine, my best friend, but besides that, it feels as though my social circle is slightly stunted.

When I moved to New York for this job, I was looking forward to getting to know my co-workers, chatting over coffee in the break room, maybe grabbing lunch with the girl from the next cubicle or something.

But days after I started there and signed the lease on my first apartment, the company announced it was giving up its corporate working space and going almost entirely remote.

Except for the top executives, all the employees shifted to working out of their apartments.

Some even left the city for cheaper rent elsewhere.

I could have left too I guess, but I'd just arrived and couldn't afford to lose my deposits.

And I really didn't want to move back home.

I had so many high hopes for living in the big city, and some of them had actually played out.

For instance, I met Spencer almost immediately. After that, I had no interest in leaving.

There were no men like him where I came from, that's for sure.

Maybe today I'll go down and work from the cafe on the corner, called Mud Pot.

It's something I do occasionally when these feelings of loneliness hit me.

The good news is, they usually don't stay for long—all it takes is one rude ogling by some weirdo on the street to make me once again immensely grateful for a remote position and the haven of our apartment.

After a quick shower and blow-dry of my hair, I pull on a pair of dark jeans and my favorite Chelsea boots before throwing on a chunky knit sweater.

It's early spring in New York City. While beautiful, it definitely still has that chill of winter lingering in the air.

Before leaving, I put on a little bit of mascara and some lip gloss, but not too much as I don't want to attract attention.

With my look situated, I slip my laptop into my bag and grab my keys, stuffing them into my pocket.

Then I'm out the door, shutting and locking it behind me.

I put my earbuds in, and I'm just about to head down the hallway, when I realize I've stepped on something.

It's an envelope.

I blink—I wasn't expecting any deliveries today.

A cursory examination of the slightly-crumpled envelope doesn't reveal the name of the sender, and there is no return address listed.

Interesting.

I've got to clock in soon, but this mysterious envelope has piqued my interest.

Have I got time?

My eyes flick down to my watch. Yeah, a couple minutes.

I unlock my door again and step back inside, letting it swing closed behind me as I grab a knife from the knife block to slice open the top of the envelope.

My heartbeat quickens as I get it open, my mind dancing with questions about what could possibly be inside.

Is it an invitation from a neighbor?

Some kind of announcement for the building's tenants?

I hope they're not raising the rent again.

The questions only grow louder as I see only a single sheet of loose-leaf paper, with what appears to be a handwritten message on it.

You don't know your husband.

CHAPTER 2
ABBY

I stare at the message, my heart attempting to climb my ribcage.

The paper is clutched in both hands as I read the sentence again.

You don't know your husband.

It's only five words. Five words that have my throat tightening and eyes rapid-blinking.

I turn the page over, but there's nothing written on the back. That ominous sentence is the entirety of the message.

I pick up the envelope again and look it over, but there's nothing to indicate who the message could've come from. My address is cleanly written, but that is all.

My gaze runs across the hastily-scribbled note again.

What do they mean, I don't know my husband?

I know exactly who he is, and that's the reason I married him.

Right?

This has to be some sort of weird prank, or something. Maybe it's not even meant for me, as there's no name listed above our address.

Despite my sensible arguments, I can't help but feel

strange about this. An uncomfortable prickling sensation grows within my chest as I stand clutching the note.

It's the ambiguity of it, that's the problem.

So little information creates so many questions.

My eyes are drawn to the windows at the other side of the apartment, which let in a crisp morning breeze.

I cross the room, the hardwood boards creaking beneath me.

Drawing the windows closed, I linger a moment to peer down at the street outside.

As if I'm in one of the suspense movies we've watched, and I'm going to see someone staring up at me, waiting to see if I've gotten their message.

Of course there's no one.

All of the passersby, so tiny from this height, have their heads buried in their phones as they walk along the streets beneath me.

My own phone buzzes, making me jump.

It's my alarm, meant to get me started on work for the day if I haven't already.

I'm still holding the note in my hand, not exactly sure what I should do with it.

Throw it away?

I stare at the paper and that disturbing phrase again.

Should I tell Spencer about this?

Maybe it's a prank from one of his buddies, though if it is, I don't get the joke.

For some reason, I make the decision not to tell Spencer, not right away anyway.

I'm not sure why, as I absolutely hate keeping things from my husband, and as far as I know, he hasn't kept anything from me.

But still, the very existence of this note suggests maybe he has. I need more time to think about it.

Maybe I don't know Spencer as well as I think I do.

My alarm goes off again–*you better really hurry now*.

Licking my lips, I hurriedly fold the note into a small square and tuck it into my jeans pocket before shooting back across the apartment.

In the kitchen area, I crumple up the envelope and toss it into the trash.

As I scoop up my purse in preparation to head out again, my peripheral vision catches on a burst of movement.

The TV—I forgot to turn it off when I left the apartment the first time.

It's the top of another news cycle, and once again, the murder is the top story. The screen is flashing images of Central Park where they found the girl's body.

There's more information now.

She's been identified as Elizabeth Waters, a graduate student at NYU. The sound is muted, but I'm still drawn to the images of the bright yellow caution tape and flashing red and blue lights.

Then the screen switches back to a news woman who addresses the viewer with a somber look on her face.

I pick up the remote and click the volume on to hear what they're saying.

"*—found in the early hours this morning by joggers, who came across the disturbing scene just before six AM,*" the news anchor says.

"*Police noted that aside from her throat having been slashed, a portion of Waters's hair appeared to have been chopped off as well, possibly by her killer.*"

My hand comes up to touch my own hair instinctively. It's long, and Spencer loves to braid it.

They flash Elizabeth's picture on the screen again, and my heart breaks for her.

What a horrible thing to have happened to such a young girl, just beginning her life.

What kind of monster could take an innocent life like that —and end it so abruptly?

It makes me so sad, but I'm not going to let it scare me about the city.

Monsters exist everywhere.

I shudder and shake my head then switch off the TV. With my purse underarm, I race out of the apartment, chest huffing as I head for the elevator.

The apartment adjacent to ours has the door open.

It belongs to Mrs. Glenn, a sweet old lady who's blind and very nearly deaf. She doesn't have any family, so I help around her house when she needs it.

Forgetting my concerns for a moment, I stick my head inside to make sure she's okay.

"Mrs. Glenn?" I call.

The older woman shuffles around the corner, hunched to the point she resembles a question mark.

"Hello dear, is it grocery day today?" she asks.

"No, that's tomorrow, remember? I'll stop by and help with that, okay?" I say gently.

"Ah, I see. I have my days mixed up. Thank you dear," she says, and then shuffles away.

I pull her door shut and then head for the elevator, my mind already back on the questions that fill it.

Mud Pot looks fairly busy today, most of the tables visible through the large front windows occupied.

I push open the door, cheeks cold and no doubt flushed from the brisk outdoor air.

The barista behind the counter recognizes me instantly.

"Morning, Abby," she says in a sweet voice.

It's Rachel, who's served me before. I'm pretty sure she's an NYU graduate student, just like Elizabeth Waters was.

"The usual?" she asks me, her brown hair bobbing around her chin as she smiles.

I glance over at her, blinking for a moment. The mysterious envelope is still front-of-mind, everything else having to take a backseat while I mull it over.

Rachel is still looking at me, waiting for an answer.

"Yes please," I manage with a thin smile.

Rachel nods, and I move toward an open two-seat table pressed up against the front window.

My purse lands with a muffled thump on the worn laminate tabletop. I pull out my laptop and take a breath, trying to get myself into work mode.

A quick glance out the window shows a chilly-looking couple chattering their way down the street, their shoulders hunched against the wind as they walk away from me.

It's warm in here though, for which I'm grateful.

I rub my hands together and turn on my laptop.

Letting out a breath, I shut my eyes and work to clear my head. Yes, the note was weird, but I can't spend all day thinking about it.

Opening up my email, I get to work.

I'm what my company calls a *customer success manager*, which is really a fancy way of saying I'm a customer service representative.

I've moved up through the ranks enough over the years that I don't answer the phones directly anymore.

My job now centers more on dealing with the bigger issues that are sent up the pipeline.

Somehow, I've managed to thrive in this position, which feels rather ironic considering I'm quite shy in person-to-person, real life interactions.

Today though, I can hardly focus at all, despite all my efforts to the contrary. My mind keeps drifting back to the note.

You don't know your husband.

I blink and discover I've been gazing out the window again, turning the mysterious message over in my mind.

Shaking my head, I force my eyes back down to my computer screen and the customer ticket in front of me.

I have to read it twice before I'm able to comprehend what's happening with this person's complaint.

Finally, I start tapping on the keys, but even then, I can't stop thinking about the strange note that was left for me. What do they want me to know?

Is there anything to know?

The spring sun breaks through the clouds and shines down on the city as it slowly emerges from its winter cocoon, drawing my attention outside once again.

There are still a few frozen piles of filthy snow on the street corners, its glorious white color long since tarnished with all sorts of soot and debris.

Even though it's midday, there aren't many pedestrians about. It seems as though the cold weather has most people staying inside. Despite being inside myself, I shiver in my thick sweater.

So much for getting any work done today. My mind is too muddled.

I'm torn between my love for Spencer and the millions of questions that have suddenly been raised by this anonymous, five-word note.

Is our relationship really this fragile?

Is it possible that it's true?

Could I really not know my own husband?

CHAPTER 3
SPENCER

Contrary to what people might think, my life is no dream.

On paper, everything seems totally perfect. I've got a great paying job, a gorgeous apartment in a prime spot in New York City, and a loving wife.

All of that isn't enough to satisfy me, as here I am on my lunch break in another woman's bed, absentmindedly braiding her hair as we giggle together.

They give me an hour at work for lunch, which is more than enough time. My assistant Jane's apartment isn't that far away from our office building.

She's nearly ten years younger than me, but it doesn't feel like it when we're together.

Some Maroon 5 song drifts lazily out of a speaker as we spoon in bed.

Eventually Jane gets up to go use the bathroom, her bare behind catching my gaze as she looks back flirtatiously.

"Should I make us some drinks?" she asks, picking up a bottle of vodka and some Cointreau.

"I thought what we just did was supposed to come *after* drinks, not before," I reply with a smirk.

Jane rolls her eyes before closing the bathroom door.

As she does, my phone buzzes on the nightstand.

It's a text from Abby.

As I see her name, I get that familiar twinge of guilt.

It's not enough to stop me today, and it hasn't stopped me in the past. Still, I can't help but feel a little sorry for her. I'm not sure what it is about her, exactly—or if it's anything about her at all.

I know Abby is a great woman.

She's exactly my type, or at least was, a decade ago.

Maybe it's just that her love feels too... *loving*.

It's hard to put into words exactly, but I almost feel oppressed by how much she loves me. Maybe that's just the guilt talking because I don't love her the same way she loves me.

Of course I can never say that to her.

I hear the sink running behind the closed bathroom door and use the opportunity to let out a fart I've been holding in for the past twenty minutes.

Some days I fantasize about getting caught, about stories of my cheating getting back to Abby.

Then I wouldn't have to be the one to tell her and break her heart. It'd already be done, already be out there. The hard part would be over.

Obviously the next step would be divorce though, and I can't have that. Not now, not ever.

If something were to happen to Abby though...well, I suppose that wouldn't be the worst thing.

If I ever did get married again, I'd have to figure out a real good lie to explain that—much like how I lied to Abby about my first wife.

Abby still has no idea what happened, and with any luck, she never will.

Maybe I'm just a bad person. My psychiatrist says all of

this stems from my narcissistic tendencies. A stupid take from such a supposedly smart man.

Narcissism–that's what my Dad was, not me. Then again, I don't have a doctorate hanging on the wall, so what do I know?

I finally work up the guts to read Abby's message. To my surprise, it's not some lovey-dovey slop that I have to grit my teeth and come up with a reply for.

Instead, it's only a few words.

Is everything OK?

My chest pangs. Why would she ask that?

Does she know about Jane?

I reread the message, my mind racing as I sit up in bed a little.

Blinking, I allow myself a breath. *Calm down*. That's just my guilty conscience talking. She's not asking about *us* being okay, she's just checking in on me as usual.

I chew my lip and fire off a thumbs-up emoji, along with some garbage about how busy the subway was.

After another second, I add that I miss her already, even as the bathroom door opens again, and Jane bounces out and leaps back into bed with me.

"Who are you texting?" she asks.

"Work thing," I reply automatically, before remembering that Jane works with me. That's the excuse I use with Abby.

Jane checks her phone then shakes her head.

"Interesting. I didn't get anything."

I wave her off. "Some upper-level stuff. No big deal."

Jane rolls her eyes. "Ooh, okay, Mr. Big Shot. How—"

I toss my phone back on the nightstand and lean in to kiss Jane before she can ask any more inconvenient questions.

She really is beautiful, even reminding me a little of my wife about five years back, when she was in fantastic shape.

Jane is obviously pleased. She giggles when my lips lock

with hers, and I feel her hands running along my back as we get back down to business again.

Once we're done, it's my turn to go to the bathroom and get myself cleaned up to return to the office. On the way down the hall, I catch sight of her calendar hanging slightly tilted on the wall.

Leaning down, I let out a chuckle as I tap a particular square where an appointment is written. Jane scowls at me.

"What, a girl can't have therapy? It's good for you, you know."

I shake my head. "No, it's not that. I actually see Dr. DeLuca, too."

What are the odds? New York City really does feel like a small town sometimes.

Our lunch break is nearly over, and I've certainly worked up quite an appetite. I'll grab something greasy off a food cart on the way back.

I step out of the bathroom adjusting my tie, because I know how much women like to see that.

Sure enough, I've got Jane's full attention as she lounges on the bed. Strangely though, the look in her eyes isn't the lustful one I expected.

"You love me, right?" she asks.

The words hang in the air as I tighten my grip on my tie.

I manage a playful grin.

"Of course I do," I say in my silkiest voice, knowing that girls love it when my voice gets a little deep and husky.

Abby sure does. My first wife loved it too.

I take a few steps towards Jane and lean down, our lips locking again. I can feel her body surge toward me and get that familiar sense of power that comes from knowing I practically own her.

I'm just about to head out, but I have to grab my phone first. It's on the bedside table across from Jane.

"I'll see you very soon," I say with a wink before tossing

my suit jacket over my shoulder and heading for the door of her dingy studio apartment.

She's got her fur coat hanging off a hook on the inside of it, which means I have to sift through the heavy swaths of fabric a moment in search of the handle.

A stir of movement at my feet makes me jump, but it's only her cat shooting between my legs before going to hide underneath one of the chairs against the kitchen island.

Once safe in its sanctuary, it hisses at me. They say cats are good judges of character.

I let out a chuckle and pull open the door, turning around to blow a kiss to Jane before letting the door shut.

When I see her later in the office, we won't even acknowledge each other.

That's the way this thing has to work. I've learned that lesson well after years of trial and error.

I don't know why I am the way I am, why I can't be happy with a wife.

It seems as though no matter what, even if I find the perfect girl—which I thought I'd done twice—sooner or later I start to get bored.

It happened the first time after a couple of years. It took longer with Abby, and for a while I thought maybe it wouldn't happen at all.

Then about a year ago, I got that itch. I'm powerless to stop it.

It's just so easy, especially knowing that Abby works completely remotely. She never sees the looks other women give me in the street or how waitresses and bartenders eye me when I order drinks.

Abby's problem is that she's too trusting, too loving.

Really, it's her fault that I do the things I do.

If she didn't make me feel so uncomfortable with all the smother-love, drowning me in it, maybe I wouldn't feel a need to escape.

CHAPTER 4
ABBY

I look up from my bench as Katherine crosses the path toward me.

Her auburn hair is pulled into a tight bun as usual, though today's wind has managed to disrupt her normally put-together appearance.

Loose strands whip about her face, getting caught in her scarf and making her lift a hand to shield her eyes from the errant pieces.

We meet up like this about every other day.

Other than the cafe, it's pretty much my only real human interaction outside of Spencer.

Today, I'm even more anxious than usual to walk and talk with Katherine.

"Sorry I'm late, got trapped in convo with a coworker nearly the entire lunch break," Katherine says with an eye-roll, "I can only say *how sweet*, and *aren't they adorable* so many times before I feel ready to snap."

"No worries," I say with a small smile as we lean in and hug.

She smells nice, like fresh flowers. A fitting scent for

spring, if the weather ever decides to acknowledge the season and warm up.

Katherine pulls back and glances around the Park with a grimace.

"We might need to pick a new walking spot. Did you see the news?"

I nod.

"Just awful. Poor girl," Katherine says as she rubs her arms with a shiver.

I almost expected to see Central Park closed off for the day when I walked over, but thankfully it wasn't.

The Park is so massive, the opposite sides of it might as well be different worlds.

Katherine and I begin our walk along the main path, shoes scuffling on the asphalt as a dry wind blows a discarded paper bag across it.

"So what's new?" she asks. "Sounded like there was something you wanted to share with me."

She sounds a little excited and definitely curious, alluding to the semi-mysterious text I sent her when confirming our meetup.

I nod, biting my lip.

I did want to tell her, could hardly wait. Now that I'm here though, I don't know what exactly to say.

Obviously I *should* tell Katherine, right?

She's become my best friend—really my only friend. I've got acquaintances, but no one other than her I feel comfortable truly sharing details of my life with.

And about *this* detail, I could definitely use some outside perspective. Otherwise, it'll eat me up entirely.

I also know that Katherine is a straight shooter, for better or worse. When we first met, her straightforward manner of speaking took me by surprise.

In fact, the first few times I saw her, I felt a little taken aback, until I understood she didn't mean anything by her bluntness. It's just her way.

"Well… I received a strange note this morning," I start.

That catches Katherine's attention immediately.

She glances over at me, her eyebrows shooting up her forehead.

"Oh? Do tell."

"It's… it was this anonymous, handwritten note. No return address or anything," I continue, stalling a little on spilling the whole story for some reason.

In spite of the cold, my palms feel sweaty. Is it because I'm nervous to hear what she's going to say?

Katherine prods me onward with an eager hand gesture, practically willing the information out of me.

"Spit it out already," she urges, "You know how much I hate to wait."

I stop walking, and she does, too, turning to face me with an expectant look on her face.

"It said I… *didn't know my husband*," I say finally, the words rushing out of me.

Katherine stares at me a moment.

"Don't know your husband? What else?"

"*You don't know your husband* is all it said," I say with a shake of my head.

Her eyes widen as she digests the message.

I can almost see the thoughts forming in her head as she whirls back toward me.

"Is Spencer cheating on you?"

I shake my head vigorously. "No way. I don't believe it."

Katherine appraises me for a moment but doesn't say anything. The silence stretches another second, and I feel the urge to speak again, to protect him from the negative opinions she must be forming.

"How could he? We're together almost every night. Besides, I know Spencer. He wouldn't."

My adamant words are supposed to dispel any doubt—whether for me or her I'm not sure. But they come out sounding more pleading than confident.

I search Katherine's face, hoping she'll agree with me and tell me there's no reason to worry.

But she doesn't seem nearly as convinced as I'd hoped. Her lips are pursed before she speaks again.

"You do say he spends a lot of time at work."

"He's very important," I reply hurriedly, my arms crossing defensively across my chest.

"I don't know, Abby. These days, it seems like you can never be too sure," Katherine says.

"I know Spencer, I *trust* him."

Still, the questioning voice in my head remains. I can feel my self-assurance weakening a little, especially in the face of someone like Katherine, who doesn't ever sugarcoat things.

Our eyes meet again, and I swallow hard. Her sympathetic expression is making my throat tighten and my eyes sting. It's obvious she thinks there's a possibility the note actually means something.

And now I can't stop all the questions from rushing in—maybe I don't want to.

What if Spencer really is cheating on me?

"Do you really think..." I begin, but I can't stand to finish the question out loud.

The implication is just too much to bear.

Katherine's cheek pulls back in a sad-looking half smile.

"Never say never, is what I've learned."

I start walking again, more to distract myself than anything else. If I stay in motion, I can't worry as much. Katherine keeps in step with me as I shake my head again and again.

"I refuse to believe it," I say, finding a little strength.

If I don't have trust in Spencer, we don't have anything.

I can't let some random note destroy what we've built together.

Beside me, Katherine seems to be sifting through her own thoughts, putting them together in new patterns. Finally she says something.

"From all you've told me, I've always thought he did seem a little too perfect."

Her hand comes out in a staying gesture. "I'm not saying he's *definitely* been unfaithful. I mean, good guys do exist... somewhere. I'm just saying you never truly know anyone."

You never truly know anyone.

It's a phrase I've heard tossed around many times, and one I'm sure I've even said a few times myself. When it comes to my husband however, I hadn't ever believed it.

I still don't.

Right?

"What should I do?" I ask Katherine.

With the chaotic mess of thoughts rushing through my head, I could really use some of her no-nonsense clarity right now.

"Should I say something to him?"

She immediately shakes her head.

Considering the robustness of her response, I decide not to share my insecure little *Is everything okay?* text to Spencer earlier this morning.

"No way," Katherine says. "If Spencer is up to something, that'll just spook him, and he'll shut down and get all careful before you can figure out the truth."

"*If* there is anything to figure out," I add quickly.

"Right," she says after a moment.

She takes a deep breath, her eyes flicking around the park conspiratorially as she gathers her thoughts.

"I say, business as usual. Maybe even extra lovey-dovey. If he doesn't reciprocate, that could be a sign he's pulled away from you. Then you start looking deeper."

I nod, taking her idea in and considering it. It won't be hard for me to dote on Spencer, considering that's what I always do.

Up until this morning, he was my whole world.

I shake myself. He still is.

Whatever the message meant, it can't be what Katherine suspects.

"Okay," I say, my teeth chattering as a blast of crisp air moves over us and seeps beneath my clothing.

"Stay strong, Abby. And tell me everything that happens."

I prop up my eyebrow. "This *is* my marriage, you know—not one of your gossip forums."

Katherine shakes her head. "Sorry, sorry. Of course. You know how I get. Just know that whatever happens, I'm here for you."

She pulls me into a hug, the two of us embracing again as I shut my eyes tight. For a moment, everything is okay.

And then we separate, and my eyes open to the world again. A world that seems a little bit harsher than it did yesterday.

I'm so grateful to have Katherine in my life, but I don't even want to imagine her needing to be *here for me*, because that implies Spencer's done something and I'll need tending-to as a result.

It makes my stomach twist just thinking about the possibility.

Katherine *has* to be wrong. This note has to be talking about something else.

If not, who did I marry?

CHAPTER 5
ABBY

I'm at the stove when Spencer finally comes home.

Sizzling before me is his favorite food, New York Strip steak with all the right seasoning. I've got the asparagus boiling in a pot on the eye beside the skillet, and it's nearly finished.

Right on time too, as Spencer steps through the door with his leather briefcase in hand.

He sniffs the air appreciatively.

"Hey gorgeous," he says with a big smile.

Immediately, I feel the knot of stress that's been growing in my stomach over the course of the day begin to unravel.

He wouldn't smile like that if he was cheating on me. He'd have to be a sociopath.

He shuts the door behind him. Then his eyes widen as he realizes what's on the stove.

"Is that—"

I nod, grinning widely as I turn off the eye and slide his precisely medium rare steak from the skillet onto a plate. It continues to sizzle even once it hits the ceramic.

Spencer loosens his tie with a big goofy grin on his face, making his way into the kitchen.

"And to what do I owe this pleasure?" he purrs.

Reassuring warmth rushes through me. "No reason. Just that I love you."

I can tell Spencer is very pleased by my choice for dinner, and that makes me happy. He comes toward me, and I get a delicious whiff of his cologne.

I rise up onto my toes, anticipating his kiss and preparing to be wrapped up in his arms again.

Things are okay. Of course they are.

Only he doesn't hug me.

Or kiss me.

Instead, he scoops up the plate and brushes past me, heading for the fridge.

"Thanks, hon. Starved," he says over his shoulder as he cracks the refrigerator door and grabs a beer.

Blinking, I try not to let the crushing weight of his casual dismissal topple my belief in him. I can see Katherine's face in my mind and hear her words, but I try to block them out.

Beer bottle in hand, Spencer makes his way over to the dining table and plops down with a heavy sigh.

He's tired, that's all. It's been a very long workday.

I can't assume he doesn't love me just because he didn't hug me. It means nothing other than what he said—he's hungry and eager to enjoy the meal I prepared for him.

Biting my lip, I grab my own plate from the counter and join him.

"How was work?" I ask.

Spencer looks up from his phone, which he's pulled out and is scrolling through. When I talk though, he instantly shuts it off and sets it down. That soothes my ruffled feathers a bit.

He's always given me his full attention, and I love that about him.

This whole thing with the note is crazy, and I'm starting to feel guilty for even considering something is wrong.

"Busy," he says, "very busy. We lost a couple people over the weekend, so now I've got to shoulder the load, which means there might be a couple late nights this week."

I nod and hurriedly stuff a bite of asparagus into my mouth. Spencer is digging into his steak, his eyes rolling back a little as he lets out a satisfied moan.

"Wow, this is really wonderful. Thanks."

I beam at the compliment. Wait until he hears my next surprise.

"I was thinking for movie night tonight, instead of that horror movie, which we both know is probably terrible, we could watch your favorite—*Fatal Attraction*."

Spencer glances up at me. He looks at me for a long moment, still chewing.

"Okay, what's going on? I thought you didn't like that movie," he says.

"I've only seen it once, but I know how much you like it, so I'm willing to give it another shot," I say.

Spencer smiles again and swallows. "Fine by me. A little classic Michael Douglas sounds mighty good. Thanks, babe."

With dinner finished, we head into the living room, and I get the movie pulled up on the streaming service.

The two of us assume our usual positions, sitting close together on the couch with a cozy blanket over our legs.

But a few minutes into it, I'm a little worried. Though I'm pressed against Spencer's side, he doesn't put his arm around me in the usual way. Then he shifts position, and I allow myself to exhale and relax a little as the comforting weight of his arm settles around my shoulders.

See? Everything's normal.

I was ridiculous for worrying he didn't love me. That note has apparently turned me into a basket case.

I know that Spencer cares deeply for me, otherwise he wouldn't have married me, right?

Taking another deep breath, I let it out slowly. I'm glad that I've settled down and moved past this.

Some silly prankster doesn't get to derail my happy marriage. We've always been happy.

In fact, I'm so sure of him that it makes me want to initiate something tonight.

I feel a little rash of goosebumps raise across my skin in excitement as I think about the new lingerie I bought. He hasn't seen it yet.

It was an impulse purchase, and I've been waiting for the right moment to show him. Tonight will be the night.

When the end credits roll, I lean over and press my lips against Spencer's as I crawl over him and straddle his lap. He kisses me back, making my heart beat faster.

I'll never get over this feeling—him kissing me, the passion I can feel behind it.

But he breaks the kiss abruptly and pulls his head back. My eyes open to see his are open as well. And they're not exactly filled with passion.

"What's wrong?"

"I'm sorry, babe, I just can't tonight. I'm so stressed out from work and everything. So tired, too."

All the excitement inside me deflates like a bouncy house in a hailstorm.

I try not to let his turning me down crush me completely, managing a small nod. "Sure. I understand."

He slides me off of his lap and heads into the bathroom, letting out a burp before shutting the door behind him.

The slam of the door echoes in my mind. I know it wasn't that loud in reality, but sitting alone on the couch, I fight back a sudden welling of tears in my eyes.

Spencer refusing me feels horrible, and I recall Katherine's words from earlier.

You never truly know anyone.

Maybe I don't know what's going on inside Spencer's mind. Maybe he really doesn't love me anymore.

I think back to when we were first married, how we could hardly keep our hands off each other. With a start, I realize it hasn't been that way for a long, long time.

I hear the sink turn on.

Spencer begins to hum a couple notes to some older Maroon 5 song while he brushes his teeth, getting ready for bed.

It feels like blinders are lifting from my eyes as I sit on the couch and stare at nothing, rubbing the thick blanket between my fingers and racking my brain for exactly how long it's been.

When was the last time Spencer initiated, and not me?

As far back as I can remember in recent memory, it's always been me.

A chill races through me as the truth of my situation begins to dawn.

When we settle into bed, Spencer mumbles *goodnight* then applies his mouth tape and rolls over without kissing me.

To me, it's the final nail in the coffin. I can excuse the other stuff, but forgetting to kiss me goodnight is the last straw.

I remain motionless beside him, a cold sensation running down the length of my body as I glance over at his head on the pillow beside me.

Could it really be true?

Could we have somehow lost touch to the point I really do not know this man anymore?

Spencer's bare back is turned to me, his shoulder rising and lowering slowly with each intake of breath. I notice an abnormally long, dark hair growing out of his back. It's much longer than all the rest.

Soon enough he's fallen asleep, even letting out a light snore despite the tape that keeps his mouth shut.

Sleep does not come for me so easily.

Instead I lie awake, my mind racing as I stare up at the ceiling for what feels like hours, running over the day's events in my mind. Finding the note. The conversation with Katherine.

As much as I don't want to believe it, it is time to face the possibility. Spencer might be cheating on me.

The note might be right.

I might not know my husband after all.

CHAPTER 6
SPENCER

The next morning is unusually quiet, but I'm not complaining.

Usually, I have to summon a few *I love you's* which is always draining and makes me feel bad, as I'm essentially lying to Abby's face.

I don't want to lie and feel like a fraud, but what else am I going to do?

When she tells me she loves me, I have to respond with the same, or she'll get upset.

Today though, it's a different story.

Abby hasn't said, *I love you* once, which means I don't have to say it, either.

She's quietly getting breakfast ready, her hair frizzy as she stands by the stove in her shapeless pajamas, working the eggs around the skillet sizzling in front of her.

I'm adjusting my tie, taking a peek in the hallway mirror as I study my jawline. Though I'm approaching my mid-thirties, and a lot of guys my age are starting to get soft, I still manage to keep my health intact.

Perks of a fast metabolism. Seeing myself fills me with a sense of pride.

Abby, on the other hand, has started to let herself go a little bit.

That might be why I'm starting to stray. If she had kept herself in better shape, maybe I would be less willing to risk it.

After all, I'm trying my hardest here, and it seems like she isn't. I guess I married the wrong woman. *Again*.

The thing is, I can't get divorced.

Half my stuff gone, the public shame of it all? No thanks.

Shannon and I were going to get divorced. At least, that's what I think she wanted to do, but of course that worked itself out.

I shake my head and back away from the mirror, running a hand through my hair as I step over to the kitchen island.

Abby is dividing up the eggs onto two plates as usual. I notice she doesn't put her plate beside mine. I look up at her.

"Is everything okay? You seem a little quiet this morning," I ask, putting as much sincerity into the words as I can muster.

Abby rubs her eyes. "Still asleep, I guess. Didn't get the best rest last night."

From the dark bags under her eyes, I can tell she isn't kidding. That explains it.

Knowing I should probably console her, I push off of the barstool seat and round the corner of the marble counter to pull her into a hug.

I feel her stiffen slightly in my arms, but a quick check of my watch tells me I don't have time to get into the reasons with her.

Maybe it's that time of the month.

Whatever's wrong, it'll have to wait—I need to hurry it up.

Breaking away from her, I return to my plate and hurriedly scarf down the eggs.

"Will you be late tonight?" Abby asks.

I rack my brain, trying to remember if my date is today or tomorrow. We're supposed to see a museum exhibit at the Met.

Obviously, I can't pull out my phone and double-check the reservations for the tickets right now.

"I might be," I say, "depending on how things move today. You know how it is."

A good answer, I think. Abby seems to buy it and turns away from me, leaving me free to grab my briefcase and suit jacket off the chair.

Finally, I'm out the door and heading down the hallway. I'm moving quickly, glancing down at my watch every few seconds as if that's going to somehow slow down time for me.

I hear the door open behind me and turn around.

Abby has her head stuck out into the hallway, looking at me. There is a strange expression on her face that I can't quite place, but I'm in such a hurry.

Why doesn't she just go ahead and say what she wants from me so I can go?

I can't quite disguise the exasperation in my voice as I ask, "Did I forget something?"

I glance meaningfully down at my briefcase and suit jacket. Nope, everything is accounted for.

"Love you," she says in a small voice.

A small knot forms in my stomach as I look back at her, my eyes coming to a stop on her face as she waits for my reply.

It kills me to lie to her, but what other choice do I have?

"I love you too," I say.

Then I tap my watch and race off toward the elevator as I hear the apartment door close gently behind me.

Abby definitely looked rough this morning. Maybe she's coming down with something. For a moment I'm even a little worried that maybe she suspects my extracurricular activities, but I quickly dismiss the thought.

I've done a great job covering my tracks. Besides, she's so in love with me she's too blind to even consider that anything could be going on behind her back.

That thought gives me another twinge of regret. It's definitely not a good thing that I'm doing to her, but I also could never divorce her.

A strange thought hits me.

No, that can't be it.

Am I waiting for what happened to my first wife to happen to Abby?

That wasn't my fault.

I was at work at the time, after all. The police confirmed it. Besides, having something happen to two wives would be a little too suspicious, no matter how strong an alibi I might have.

I set my brow in determination as I board the elevator. No, it doesn't have to get that far.

Somehow, I'll manage to make everything okay. I pull out my phone and scroll through my emails, confirming that today is indeed the day for the museum trip.

I check and make sure I've got both of the tickets then fire off a message to Caroline telling her how excited I am about the exhibit.

My phone buzzes again as a text comes in, though this one isn't from her—or Abby.

It's from the cute girl I met while grabbing coffee earlier this week. She's free later this week—perfect.

Sometimes it gets hard to keep track of all of my lies. Abby has no idea about Caroline—or Jane, who in turn has no idea about my newest fling.

As far as Jane knows, I'm going through a divorce.

The new girl knows nothing at all.

She has no idea I'm married, as when I met her, I didn't have my ring on.

The moment I got into line, I noticed her in front of me. I

had no plans to meet anyone new, considering how many girls I'm already juggling-but she was just my type.

I put my hand in my jacket pocket, casually slid my ring off my finger, and prepared to approach her.

She smiled so brightly as I came up and introduced myself.

The smile got even bigger when she glanced down and saw there was no ring on my finger, telling me I had done the right thing.

Five minutes later, I walked out with her number on a napkin.

Only issue was, I got so caught up in flirting I forgot to ask her to put her name down as well, which means I have absolutely no idea what it is.

I'm not sure what it is about me, why I can't stick to just one woman. Maybe I've just got too much love to give, and one person isn't enough to hold it all.

I almost chuckle at that notion.

More likely, it's the thrill of meeting someone new, someone who doesn't know my past—a past that will inevitably come to light once I've known a person long enough.

It happened with Abby, and maybe *that's* why I started to drift away from her.

I can tell I'm getting to that place with Jane now too. Sure she's hot, and I love gingers, but soon enough she'll discover the more… unsavory parts of me.

Try as I might, it always comes out.

And once it does, once they know, I just can't look at them the same anymore.

With New Girl however, it's a fresh start.

I love those. I respond to her message, telling her I'm looking forward to seeing her, then tuck my phone back into my pocket.

I'm a smart guy, and I'm sure I'll find a way to get her name without asking for it somehow.

No message from Abby so far today, which is also a little out of character.

Usually, I don't escape the building without my phone buzzing with a message from her telling me how much she loves me.

Honestly, it's a relief.

It feels good not to be suffocated with love for a change. Maybe she's finally settling down now too.

I exit our building and stride forward, shoulders back as I confidently take on the world ahead of me.

I really do have it all—a wife who cooks at home, a fun girlfriend who adores me, and a girl who could be my next new fling.

After all I've had to go through in the past, life is now looking up for me, that much is for sure.

I have to hold myself back from feeling *too good*, though, as a sense of déjà vu envelopes me.

I've had this feeling before when I was with Shannon, just before everything changed. I had a girlfriend on the side then, too, and was feeling on top of the world.

Then Shannon started to nag me, started to grow suspicious.

Soon enough, what happened happened, and then the police were everywhere.

The scrutiny I was put under was a stressor in and of itself.

No man could continue to perform at the top of his game under those conditions. I even had to put my relationship with my girlfriend on hold during the whole investigation.

So yes, I must be careful.

Abby can't find out, and I need to remain level-headed.

I can't have a repeat of what happened with my first wife.

CHAPTER 7
ABBY

There is a war going on in my mind.

I'm torn between searching Spencer's tablet and trusting him. The apartment is quiet around me. The only noise is the distant honking from far below on the city streets.

Spencer is no doubt already at work by now, busy and distracted. I glance over at the tablet lying on the couch beside me.

Spencer doesn't know it, but I've seen him type his passwords enough times that they've been ingrained into memory.

He's never been one to try and hide them anyway, which I used to take as a comforting sign of his loyalty.

Do I dare chance a peek? Everything changes if I do.

The shrill buzzing of my phone jars me, making me blink. It's Mrs. Glenn calling from next door. I gulp down a breath of oxygen to calm myself before answering.

"Yes, Mrs. Glenn?" I ask.

"Hello dear," Mrs. Glenn says, her voice shaking a little, "I hate to be a bother, but I think groceries are to be delivered soon, and–"

Oh my gosh.

I've been so caught up in my own drama, I completely forgot about my weekly routine with Mrs. Glenn, even after our conversation yesterday. Hurriedly I check my watch.

Still a few minutes until the scheduled delivery.

"Mrs. Glenn, I'm so sorry, I totally forgot. I'll be over in a second," I say, my cheeks burning a little.

Apparently a single sentence sent from an anonymous note is enough to throw my whole life off.

Poor Mrs. Glenn is sitting in there all alone, wondering if I've abandoned her.

I run my palms down the length of my pants and then grab Mrs. Glenn's key from the kitchen drawer before casting one last glance at Spencer's tablet.

Part of me is grateful for this excuse not to make the decision just yet.

A second later I've got Mrs. Glenn's door unlocked, and step inside. She's in her usual spot in the living room, hunched over in her recliner with the television loudly playing the QVC channel.

Her blindness and advanced age hasn't done anything to quell her interest in home shopping, a thought that warms me.

I open the door and step inside to ring the chime on the wall that alerts my neighbor that she has visitors.

"Is that you, dear?" she croaks.

"Yes, Mrs. Glenn, it's Abby," I say, projecting my voice.

Mrs. Glenn's apartment is a similar layout to ours, though hers actually has a second bedroom while ours does not.

She's kind enough to let us use it for storage, which saves us a small fortune by not having to rent a storage unit in the city.

"How are you feeling today?" I ask as I bend over and inspect the fridge.

"Come again?"

I clear my throat and speak up. "I asked how you are feeling today."

"Oh. As good as one can, I suppose," comes the frail reply.

A knock at the door pulls my head out of the fridge. Food delivery, right on time.

I move down the small hallway to the front door and pull it open to be greeted by bags of groceries, the delivery guy already making a beeline for the elevator.

It's mostly microwaveable meals, which I've insisted aren't healthy but Mrs. Glenn has been having for decades.

She is eighty-nine after all, so maybe she knows something I don't.

I get the food put away as Mrs. Glenn pushes up out of her recliner with a groan. She has her white cane out to feel in front of her as she makes her way toward me in the kitchen.

"Would you be so kind as to put one of those into the microwave for me, dear?" Mrs. Glenn says.

"Of course, Mrs. Glenn, I'd be happy to. Anything else I can do for you, while I'm here?"

I'm stalling, because I know what waits for me in my apartment.

The choice I have to make.

"No, no, I won't keep you. Thank you for being so kind and helping an old woman," Mrs. Glenn says as she shuffles past me.

She's so tiny and hunched that she only comes up to my chest. I get her meal into the microwave, and then I can't put it off anymore.

Back in my apartment, I sit on the couch with my lip between my teeth.

With a shaking hand, I reach over and pick up Spencer's tablet.

If I do this, there's no going back.

I'll have invaded my husband's privacy, which is a horrifying thought. Even more horrifying is the idea that I'll actually find something. My stomach starts rolling in waves that have me feeling nauseous.

The burning curiosity intensifies until it overpowers the nausea and uneasy sense of guilt.

I can't *not* look.

With a trembling hand, I tap in his password. The tablet unlocks.

It's hooked up to his phone as well, which means all of his apps and text messages are shared between the two devices.

The first thing I do is tap on the text message icon. My heart leaps up into my throat as the list of texts appears, though I feel my anxiety lessen as I look through the names.

There's mine, toward the top of the list.

Below that are a few names I know from his work. I sift through the conversations, but they all appear to be entirely work related.

I'm starting to breathe a little easier now.

But then the guilt over doubting Spencer grows larger and heavier, and my conscience starts to gnaw away at me. Of course he isn't cheating.

He loves me. I'm the one who's sketchy, sneaking through my husband's texts.

As I'm about to shut down the tablet, however, it buzzes, and a notification appears.

It's a text of some kind, but not through the native text messaging app on the phone. I stare at the words, feeling my body go numb.

Can't wait for tonight ;), it reads.

That is most definitely *not* work related.

I tap on it before it has a chance to disappear, and I'm taken to an app that I don't recognize. The icon for the app is a calculator, but there's nothing math-related inside.

It's when I notice just how many conversations there are and with how many different women that I begin to spiral.

Whatever app this is, it's clear Spencer didn't want me knowing about it.

I've never seen any other messages like this either, which tells me that Spencer must have had notifications turned off.

Tears prick at the corner of my eyes as I scroll through the ongoing conversations. There are so many, but with my head spinning like this, I'm having trouble even understanding what I'm looking at.

It's just so awful.

This is *not* the Spencer I know.

No married man should be on a dating app like this. I tap to open the first message.

It's a conversation with some woman named Caroline, who had been the one to message him while I happened to have the tablet unlocked.

Her flirty message sits at the bottom, waiting for a response from my husband. Scrolling back up through their previous messages makes my chest ache.

Witty banter back-and-forth. Innuendos.

It looks like they are going to some show tonight at the Metropolitan Museum of Art.

I can hardly breathe as I exit out of the app and navigate over to his email. If it's true, he'll have bought tickets.

There.

Two tickets for the Met. My heart stutters as I stare numbly at the confirmation email.

My husband didn't mention anything about this show to me. He knows how much I love museums, and he's never asked me to go with him even once.

He chose this random woman over me.

I fall back to the couch, my body sinking through it as I begin to spin out. I feel dizzy. I can't catch my breath.

Our whole relationship is a lie.

Spencer has been talking to not just one woman outside our marriage, but many.

He's taking one to the Met tonight.

Time seems to speed up as I throw myself back at the tablet and swipe through the other messages in a sort of delirious haze, discovering that this is not a new occurrence.

In fact, it looks like it's been going on for nearly six months.

Almost half a year Spencer has been messaging other women, and I've had absolutely no idea.

If it weren't for that mysterious note, I wouldn't have suspected a thing.

My mind returns to the message left for me in the unmarked envelope that kicked this whole thing off. Who could have sent it?

Who knew all this about my husband, when I, the woman who lives with him every day, didn't?

My thoughts scream inside my head as I open messages at random. My eyes swim with tears when I get to a photo of a woman wearing almost nothing as she poses in front of a dirty bathroom mirror.

It's from the neck down, so I can't see her face, but it's clear from the body that she's much younger than me.

I feel sick.

Even worse is my husband's responses to these sexy messages—heart eye emojis, followed by one with sweat dripping down the face as he asks for more.

My chest splits in two, and overwhelm threatens to sink me.

Spencer has been lying to me. Faking every moment of us together.

While I hugged him, slept beside him, looked lovingly into his eyes, was he thinking of someone else?

Another thought rocks me.

I know he's emotionally stepped out on me at the very least, but has he actually cheated?

A sob racks my chest, which is so tight I literally have to

gasp for air. A shaking finger opens message after message as tears drop down onto the screen.

I don't know. I can't tell how far it's gone. Some of the dating app conversations end with the girls offering their phone numbers, but Spencer must have deleted some of the messages.

This desperate search in my frantic state of mind provides nothing conclusive, and that's almost worse than the rest of it.

The not-knowing.

Is it just messaging, or even more than that?

Another sob rises up within me, coming from somewhere deep as my face drops into my hands.

A ding sounds from the tablet, jarring me. This one is a normal text, coming from someone at work. I watch in real time as Spencer replies.

I suck in a breath. Spencer is on his phone *right now*.

Oh no. My mind races. Will he be able to see that I've been snooping?

If he found out that I'd been looking into him, what would he say?

All I know is that I don't want him to know that *I* know just yet. I turn off the tablet in a hurry and toss it to the side. It's too early, and all of this is too much.

I need help. I need someone to tell me what's supposed to come next.

I grab my phone, hardly able to type in my passcode as tears roll down my face.

My mind is wild, completely unchained.

All of this is too horrible to handle alone, completely overwhelming.

I've got to meet with Katherine. She'll know what to do. And she was right.

You never really do know anybody.

My husband has lied to my face for months on end. He's

been messaging with multiple women, some of whom look at least a decade younger than me.

I truly don't know the man I married at all.

CHAPTER 8
ABBY

Katherine pulls me into a hug as I sob into her shoulder.

I miraculously managed to keep it together on the subway ride over, but I can't anymore. I don't want to break down into pieces in this bar, but I literally can't help myself.

It feels like my whole world has come crashing down around me. I don't know anything for certain anymore, and Katherine's supportive arms are the only things that are keeping me standing.

"I'm so sorry," she says as she holds me tight.

I grip onto her coat as another snot-filled sob rises up.

My eyes meet another person's momentarily, but they avert their eyes in a hurry as they move past us.

"You're going to get through this," Katherine continues.

"But how," I fire back as I pull away from her and wipe my nose.

Spencer was supposed to be my final, my checkmate.

From the minute I first laid eyes on him, I *knew* he was the one for me. It was like something out of a cheesy rom-com, only this time it was real.

Or at least I'd thought it was.

Katherine leads me to a wooden bar booth and slides into one side. I collapse onto the bench opposite her with a defeated sigh, landing hard.

"Why is it always me," I ask, the words burning my throat.

Somehow, I always seem to be the one getting the worst in relationships. Ever since I was a little girl. I hate to catastrophize, but at this point, there's really no other way to look at it.

I've told Katherine about my previous relationships, so she's aware of my less-than-stellar history when it comes to guys.

"I'd do anything for the person I love—all I ask is the same in return, is that really so hard?" I ask with a sniffle.

Katherine bites her lip as she looks out the window beside us. "You've got a lot of love to give, Abby, and I think guys can sense it. Some of them are happy to take advantage of that."

Maybe she's right. Maybe it's my stupid sense of wanting to love and be loved.

I thought Spencer was different. He didn't try to take advantage of my hopeless romantic side like all the rest.

In fact, he seemed perfect in every way. Only now do I realize the folly of that statement.

No one is truly perfect.

Everyone has secrets.

I let out a sniffle and start digging through my pockets to find a tissue so I can stop wiping my nose with my sleeve. I might be pathetic, but I don't have to be gross as well.

I'm embarrassed to see that my tears have wet the shoulder of Katherine's jacket, too.

Thankfully she doesn't comment on that. Instead, she reaches into her own pocket and pulls out a tissue, which I accept.

She's always so prepared.

I'll bet she could've seen a guy like Spencer cheating from a mile away, if she were the one with him.

A few patrons at the bar glance over at me but don't say anything, minding their own business in typical New York fashion.

We're at our favorite cocktail bar, a quiet place in Chelsea that we've been coming to for months. It's too cold to walk around outside today, but I don't think I'd be up for it even if it wasn't.

Every step I take feels shaky, like the very ground beneath me might give way at any moment.

"What should I do?" I ask miserably, my head sinking down into my palms.

The bartender comes over with a couple of Cosmopolitans but pauses as he catches sight of my wretched state. His eyes shoot over to Katherine, who nods reassuringly.

The bartender leaves the drinks on the table and scoots away without another word.

Katherine reaches over and gives my hand a small squeeze.

"Well, for starters, you should probably drink this," she says with a sympathetic smile.

I lift my head and take a sip of the Cosmo. The vibrant, citrus-y drink does taste wonderful, but it's not nearly strong enough to dull the level of pain I'm in right now.

"How could I have been so *blind*," I moan, my throat tight.

"We always are, when we love someone," Katherine replies.

"But I truly thought he loved me too. I mean, I really believed it. What did I do wrong?"

"Abby," Katherine says sharply.

The authoritative tone of her voice brings my eyes up to meet hers.

"You did nothing wrong. I don't want to hear you blaming

yourself for a second about a man cheating. The only one who's responsible for Spencer's behavior is Spencer."

I appreciate Katherine's words, but they don't fill me with very much confidence.

Part of me knows what she's saying is true.

But another part of me—the scared little girl who just wants to be loved—says that it *was* somehow my fault, and that's the most crushing part.

I've loved Spencer as hard as I possibly could, and it wasn't enough.

"You know what they say, once a cheater, always a cheater," Katherine is saying, bringing me back to reality.

"Well, I don't know for sure if he was actually cheating," I toss out weakly.

My friend gives me a hard look. "Emotional cheating *is* cheating, in my book. You really think he was sexting all those women and didn't end up sleeping with one of them? Plus, why are you even trying to defend him?"

"Because I *love* him," I insist, the words bubbling up and out of me with more force than I meant to give them.

People look over momentarily at the raising of voices before shifting back to their own conversations. When I glance back over apologetically at Katherine, she's already apologizing first.

"Sorry, sorry. You know how I am—blunt to a fault. I didn't mean—"

"It's okay," I say with a wave of my hand, "I know you're right. I just... I'm having trouble accepting it, I think."

Katherine nods as she glances toward the window again, then her eyes come back to meet mine. She looks like she's bracing for a slap, wincing as she asks the next question.

"You know, all this makes me wonder if this isn't the first time he's stepped out on a marriage. You mentioned he was married previously, right?"

I tense a little as I always do when Spencer's first marriage is brought up. Now though? Maybe it really is time to talk about it.

"Yeah, he was," I say slowly.

"Well, maybe reach out to her? Might really help your confidence to confirm Spencer was cheating on her, too. Then you'll know it wasn't anything to do with you, just his own dirtbag self," Katherine says.

I squirm a little in my seat, taking long enough to reply that Katherine's attention is pulled from the window and centers back on me.

"What?" she asks.

Here's the thing... when I first met Katherine, Spencer and I had already been married for a couple years.

The past was in the past, so I suppose I breezed over a couple of the details in regard to his first marriage.

"Abby, what is it?" Katherine repeats.

I chew my lip, knowing what her response will be to what I say next. It's the usual response when I tell people the truth about my husband's first wife.

"Well, I can't reach out to his first wife, Shannon, because... she's disappeared."

Katherine's eyes widen in alarm as she stares at me blankly from across the booth.

"Uh, what?" she asks, the grip on her cocktail glass tightening.

When she recovers, she leans forward and speaks in a harsh whisper.

"*Disappeared*? Abby, what are you talking about?"

"It's like I said. She disappeared a few years into their marriage. Filled a suitcase and hasn't been heard from since," I say.

"And that's from what, the police?" Katherine asks.

I can tell from her tone she's not going to let this go.

Then again, maybe I shouldn't either. I sit up a little straighter and nod in reply.

Katherine scoffs. "I don't know why you didn't tell me this before. All this talk about how perfect he is, and now I'm hearing that his first wife *disappeared*?"

I shift back and forth, unable to get comfortable. My eyes are drawn to the bar's front door as it opens, admitting several new patrons and a chorus of joyful laughter that feels out of place in light of our serious conversation.

"Did they look at Spencer as a suspect?" Katherine continues.

She's reminiscent of a detective herself as she asks these questions.

"Yeah, but he was released. There was no evidence of a crime, and he was at work during the window she went missing. The police confirmed it, Katherine," I say.

She eyes me from across the table. "And you believe that?"

I throw up my hands. "That's what Spencer told me. He swore it. Plus, the police checked his alibi, and it cleared. He was telling the truth."

Katherine shakes her head after swallowing another sip of her drink. "Well, we know he has no issue with lying to you. Not so far-fetched to think he'd figure out a way to lie to the police, too."

As much as it hurts to admit, she might be right. Spencer has been lying to me, and I had no idea.

The worst part is, he did it so easily.

He did it without me even having an inkling that he was being deceptive.

Katherine seems to see the gears turning in my head as she sits back. She catches my gaze and holds it before she speaks.

"Makes you wonder what else he could've lied about. The question I'm asking now is, what *really* happened to Shannon?"

CHAPTER 9
SHANNON
SEVEN YEARS AGO

Our marriage started off so well.

I think that's what lured me into such a sense of complacency.

The first year was one of the most blissful of my life. I literally couldn't remember a time I was ever happier.

Everyone I knew got sick of the giddy social media posts, the constant bragging about him, but I just couldn't contain it.

Then something changed. I'm not really even sure how to describe it exactly… but it was like a switch flipped in Spencer.

Even now, as I watch him over the top of my coffee mug, I can tell he is different.

There isn't any one thing in particular that I could point to if I were asked.

And yet—Spencer is definitely changed.

He doesn't hug me with the same affection as before. Not as tightly, and not for as long. Even during intercourse, and after when he whispers in my ear that he loves me, there is something missing.

He flashes me that smile he knows I love each and every

day, like before, but a wife knows. Something is different, I'm sure of it.

Spencer clears his throat as he steps out of the bedroom, tightening his tie with his chin tilted slightly up.

"Looks like tonight might run late, okay babe? So just… order out if you want."

I take another sip of my burning coffee as I nod. The mug warms my hands and gives me something to grip onto.

It also gives me the strength to say what I say next.

"Do you still love me?"

My question hangs in the air as I sit on the couch, watching Spencer's back for a moment before he turns around to face me.

When he does turn around, he's no longer messing with his tie.

He lets out a short laugh as he goes to the fridge. "What are you talking about?"

My eyes fall to his left thumb, which picks at his nails while he opens the fridge door with his right hand. It's a tic he only has when he's nervous. Which isn't often.

He gives another chuckle and reaches in for something, but I don't answer him. He pulls out the milk and turns around, eyeing me with that beguiling smile of his.

Another wave of warm courage surges through me, transferred from the coffee to my veins. I manage to hold his eye contact until our gazes feel locked.

As I do, I can see that confidence in Spencer's smile waver just for a millisecond. But it's enough. I know.

Before he even says a word, I *know*.

I can tell by the faltering of his smile that he sees I understand now, too.

"Shannon," he says, a pink flush coming to his face.

The milk jug is lowered quickly to the granite countertop, his breakfast prep forgotten as he moves across the room toward me.

Hot tears threaten to overflow the corners of my eyes, though I *don't* want to cry. Not here, not now in this vital moment of truth.

Where is that strength I had just moments ago?

Spencer's shiny dress shoes squeak as he approaches the couch and sits on the cushion beside me. Gone is the smile, replaced with tight lines of worry across the face I thought I knew so well.

There's another question I know I need to ask now, but I seriously don't know if I want to hear the answer.

"Did you… have you…." I begin, my voice quivering.

The coffee mug scalds my palms as I clutch onto it, but the pain is good. It grounds me. Keeps me from falling apart right in front of Spencer.

He doesn't say anything but lowers his head, and my chest tightens. My husband takes a couple of short breaths as I struggle to find my own. His non-answer *is* an answer.

He's cheated on me.

A million questions thunder through my skull. When? With whom? Where?

Here in our apartment? Once, twice?

A regular thing?

The horror of all the potential answers comes crashing down at once, my mouth opening then closing then opening again in silence, wordless with shock and pain.

How could he do this to me—to us?

I don't know what I'm expecting Spencer to do next, but he's still sitting there with his chin buried in his chest, taking these strange, shallow breaths.

When he finally does raise his head, his face is flushed a deep red.

A loud sob barrels out of him, making me jump a little at the sudden rush of anguish.

Tears glisten in his red-rimmed eyes as he pulls himself

closer to me on the couch. The expensive fabric crinkles beneath his weight.

As he moves toward me, his shoe knocks over his briefcase.

It lands with a loud thwack, but he doesn't even look.

Instead, his eyes are locked on mine as he begins to speak, the words breathless and rushed.

They pour out of him like water from a faucet turned on full stream.

"Shannon please—"

"I don't know what—what came over me—"

"I've been a fool, an absolute idiot—"

"The temptation was too strong, and I—"

He goes on and on. All of it washes over me, his pleading and begging and reasoning, as I remain nearly motionless. My back is so straight and stiff, it's like I'm wearing a brace as he continues babbling, the tears streaming down his face now.

"Shannon, I-I love you, I made a mistake. Please… please forgive me?" he finishes finally.

Spencer is practically bawling now, with these big heaving sobs that have his chest rising and falling. His handsome face shines with tears and mucus that's begun to run down out of his nose.

His hot breath lands on my cheek, but I hardly register it.

It's like my nerve endings have all burned off, leaving me numb and unfeeling. Spencer smears his hand across his nose before another powerful sob leaves his throat.

My own throat feels like it's been torn out, leaving me unable to speak.

I'm frozen, utterly unable to react. Unable to do a single thing but remain sitting here, back straight and eyes boring down into my steaming coffee.

Suddenly Spencer throws himself backward with such force that I'm snapped out of my stupor.

What is he doing?

He's launched himself off the couch, landing on his back on the floor. His head makes contact with the hardwood with a sickening thud.

"I messed it all up, I messed it all up, I messed it all up," he shrieks over and over, his words babbling and incoherent.

He's thrashing around wildly, pounding at the floor with his fists closed tight. The scene reminds me of a toddler's temper tantrum, only it's far more disturbing to witness from a full-grown adult.

As he's flailing, one of his hands strikes the sharp metal corner of the coffee table, slicing open the skin on his left palm.

Blood pours out of the wound, but Spencer doesn't stop, just keeps flailing and repeating the words which have risen to a near-shout now as he slams the back of his head repeatedly against the floor.

Blood spews from the wound on his hand, splattering the white leather of the couch and shaking me entirely out of my stupor.

"Please… stop," I say, tears falling freely down my own face now.

Spencer ceases his frantic, jerking movements instantly, his bloodshot eyes finding mine.

He's panting, wild-eyed and desperate. Then he sits up, gets to his feet, and within seconds, he's once again seated beside me on the couch.

"Shannon, please forgive me. Please, please, please, please," he says, his voice barely above a choked whisper.

Tears continue to roll down my face as I stare hard at the coffee again. I'm gripping the mug so tightly I'm afraid the ceramic might just shatter.

I'm no longer just upset. I'm in shock. And I'm terrified.

I've never seen behavior like that from anyone over the age of two, and certainly not from Spencer.

Who is this person who looks like my husband but who, in this moment, is utterly unrecognizable?

He continues to plead with me, his bloodied hand snaking over to scoop up one of mine.

It's slippery as he clutches tight to my limp fingers.

"Baby, please. I made a mistake. I promise I won't ever again, you hear me? Ever, ever–ever–ever–ever."

He's whispering the promises into my ear, trying to pour his words—and his will—directly into me.

He wants me to say something. Do something. I still can't move.

Finally, and with tremendous effort, I manage the smallest nod—nearly imperceptible except for the fact that Spencer's face is mere inches from mine.

He sees the gesture and pulls away with a sigh, thanking me over and over and over.

"Thank you–thank you–thank you–thank you–" he repeats, pulling my now-bloody hand up to his mouth to kiss it and rub it.

Then he grabs me and pulls me into a hug, spilling my coffee over the both of us as the cup is jostled and I'm unwillingly wrapped up in his arms.

He's still babbling into my shoulder, the wetness of his tears dampening my t-shirt.

"Thank you, baby. I can't get divorced. I can't lose you. I don't know what I'd do…"

But he doesn't understand.

I have not forgiven him.

My nod was not for him. It was a moment of decision for myself. Permission. A declaration that I deserve better, than I can exist on my own without my husband.

That I can leave him, that I'll be better off without him.

For as he's just shown me with this shocking outburst, I don't know the man I'm married to like I thought I did. I *never* would have thought Spencer was capable of such an unhinged display, such sudden violence and complete loss of self-control.

Thrashing around like that, he was like an animal—or a person so demented he's capable of literally *anything*, no matter how unthinkable.

A chill runs from my scalp to my tailbone and spreads throughout my body as Spencer continues to hold me tightly against his chest.

It feels like I'm in the arms of a complete stranger.

I don't know my husband. At all.

I don't know what he's capable of.

If he would do that to his own body… what might he do to me?

I need to get out before it's too late, because if I don't, I'm afraid something terrible is going to happen to me.

CHAPTER 10
ABBY

It's been hours, and we're still here at the bar.

The drinks have flowed to the point I'm unsure if I'm going to be able to walk home straight without tipping over into the street.

In my defense, there really isn't a rational response to learning your husband has been doing bad deeds behind your back, for months on end.

The alcohol burns my throat going down, but I welcome this sensation. It's a distraction from the thoughts that ravage my brain, all of them grappling for precedence as I struggle to piece together the shrapnel that is my life.

At this very moment, Spencer is probably out there walking the halls of the Met, arm-in-arm with some girl named *Caroline*.

The thought makes me sick, the drink I've just slurped down threatening to make a return appearance.

I push the empty cocktail glass away from me and chew my lip. My cheeks feel hot. Katherine, who had been saying something, stops.

"You okay, Ab? Like, obviously you aren't okay, but I mean, like, physically?"

I glance up at her, my vision slightly blurred. Tears or alcohol, I'm not sure.

"No. And it isn't the drinks—how could I have been so naive? I let my dirty, cheating husband make a total fool out of me," I say, feeling yet another round of hot tears gather at the corners of my eyes.

I shouldn't have had so much to drink. Katherine points a finger at me. She's drunk, too.

"Like I said, it's not your fault. The question now is… what are you going to do about it?"

There's a fire in her eyes at what he's done. That should stir something in me too, but despite everything, somehow I don't feel the same way.

At the thought of getting revenge, which Katherine clearly is alluding to, all the strength seems to wash out of my system.

Some part of me still loves Spencer more than I can imagine, and I hate that.

How is it possible that he's able to run around and cheat on me without a second thought, and I'm sitting here, still hopelessly, madly in love with him, even after learning the truth?

"Love is a horrible thing," I say.

"This is why you're going to get your revenge. Total and complete revenge," Katherine says over a burp.

I drop my head into my folded arms on the tabletop.

"How?" I ask through my fingers. "I just… I thought we were the only ones for each other."

My friend chews her lip as she sits back in the booth. The bar traffic has picked up around us as the evening has deepened, which in turn has raised the noise level enough that I no longer feel like I'm giving a presentation to the place about my ruined marriage.

Or, maybe it still seems that way, and I'm just too intoxicated now to notice.

Suddenly Katherine lurches forward. The fire in her eyes is even brighter.

"I've got it. I know how to make him regret everything."

I suck in a wad of saliva and straighten myself up, rubbing my hand across my eyes.

Katherine licks her lips. "Screenshots. Of everything. All the proof of him talking to other women."

The mere idea of that is enough to make my stomach turn over again, but I steel myself and give her my full attention.

"Print it all out, hide it somewhere," she says. "It'll be your secret weapon, so even if Spencer tries to delete everything to cover his tracks, you'll have proof to take to the best divorce lawyer in the city."

My vision swims again.

Going to court, splitting our assets, having to move out of the apartment. All those prying eyes into our private life.

It fills me with an overwhelming sense of dread as I pick at my ragged fingernail. I tend to bite them when I'm drinking.

"What's wrong?" Katherine asks.

"I don't know if I can even think about a divorce just yet," I croak.

"Besides, just because he's texting other women doesn't mean he's sleeping with them. No proof of that," I add weakly.

Katherine's lips come together in a hard line. I can tell she wants to speak her mind but is also weighing the fact that my emotions are all out of whack due to the alcohol.

"Actually, you're right," she says bluntly, surprising me.

I blink.

"Proof of actual infidelity would make for a much stronger case. You need to follow him, see where he goes, catch him in the act."

My hands come up in front of me, palms out in a *slow down* gesture. I only found out yesterday about all of this. I still need some time to process the trauma. Then I can decide with a level, *sober* head what my next step should be.

"Abby, don't you want to know for certain?" Katherine presses.

My teeth tug at the corner of my lip as her words sink into me.

It is true—despite my hanging onto a feeble sense of hope, despite insisting I'm not ready to make any sort of permanent moves, the question of how far Spencer's betrayal goes is eating me alive.

It'll keep doing that until I take some action.

"I'll tell you what I want to know for certain," Katherine says, "everything there is on his first wife, Shannon?"

I nod, which makes my stomach twist even more. That's a whole other facet to this that I hardly even have the capacity to think about.

"At the very least, you *need* to get copies of the incriminating evidence against him, in case he somehow gets wise to the idea that you've found him out," Katherine insists.

She leans forward over the table, making sure she has my full attention. "If he deletes things, it'll just make everything harder, you understand? Regardless of what you end up wanting to do."

My eyes squeeze shut for a moment. In my mind, I see Spencer holding hands with the Met girl, the two of them laughing like they don't have a care in the world. I open my eyes and let out a breath.

"Okay. Okay, enough of this. I do need the truth—all of it," I say.

The statement sends a spark of energy tingling down my spine as Katherine slaps the tabletop.

"There she is," she yells with a grin.

I don't share quite the same level of enthusiasm, but there's still a recognizable buzz within me, spurred on by the image of my husband with a younger woman.

"Okay then. You go home, print everything out. Photos, texts, all of it. He'll never be able to deny those conversations happened—because you know how men like to deny everything... until faced with cold, hard evidence," Katherine says.

I manage a weak smile. It's a plan. And in my current state of freefall, it's a life vest, too.

"While you do that, I'm going to dig into Shannon," my friend says. "I know you love him and believe what he told you about her, but I watch enough true crime to suspect there's more to that story than Shannon simply up and leaving."

That sobers me a little. "What are you going to do?"

Katherine flashes me a smile as she rubs her hands together.

"Oh, Abby. You know me. I'm obsessed with this stuff. Forums, videos, podcasts, all of it. I have my ways. If something shady is up, I'll find it."

I try to put a smile on my face.

I truly don't know if I could handle her finding out something, but the care she is showing for me is endearing.

Horribly embarrassing to admit, but if it weren't for Katherine, I'd be a puddle of snot and tears right about now.

Katherine seems to sense my thoughts and reaches across the table to give my hand a squeeze.

"You're stronger than you think, Abby. You'll get through this, I know you will."

"Thanks," I say with a sniffle.

It's about time to be heading home—especially since I need to get those screenshots before Spencer comes back from his date. Ugh. My *husband* is out on a *date.*

"Remember the plan," Katherine says as we embrace.

We stumble a half-step to the left due to our drunken state but manage to remain upright.

"I'll call you or something if I end up finding anything out, okay?" she says as we separate.

I nod and sniffle again.

Katherine pulls me in for one more hug. "Love you, Ab. Text me if you need anything."

We part ways, and I head up the street. The brisk wind slapping me across the face helps to keep me alert enough to walk back to the apartment without too much trouble.

It's empty as I go inside.

Spencer is still out there with that girl, but I don't know for how much longer. I picture him smiling and laughing and kissing her, and it nearly makes my legs buckle.

After such a long, cold walk, I no longer feel the alcoholic stupor I'd been in while at the bar with Katherine. But as it dissipated, it seems to have taken my willpower to enact this plan with it.

I'm no longer sure I'm strong enough to do what I vowed to do. Or sober enough.

I cast a longing glance at my bed. It would be so nice to just fall into it and pull the blankets over my head, hide from the world and let all this disappear into the oblivion of sleep.

Then I visualize Katherine's disappointed face as I tell her I didn't get the evidence, and it spurs me on past the bedroom toward the bathroom sink.

A cold splash of water across my face snaps me into reality.

Time to take control, like she said.

Retrieving the tablet, I hastily open up the app once again.

Inside, I see the offensive pictures and am crushed all over again. There are so many of them, so much revolting proof of my husband's lack of love for me.

I take screenshots of everything, cognizant of the fact that if Spencer were to check his images on his phone right now, he would see all the screenshots too. I'll delete them as soon as I'm done—I just need to remember to do it.

Once I collect all the screenshot evidence, I email it to myself and begin printing the screenshots before deleting the images off of the tablet. Finally, I delete my emails from Spencer's Sent folder.

The printer chugs along beside me, whirring as each piece of proof slides out.

I wish it would go faster. All I need is for my husband to walk in while the ink is still warm on his infidelity.

Once all the messages and pictures are printed, I swipe them off the tray and hold them up. I know I shouldn't look at them again, shouldn't obsess over them, but I can't help myself.

Why them, and not me?

The question burns my heart like the vodka in those drinks did my throat.

These women are beautiful. Fit and toned in ways I struggle to achieve these days.

A sudden noise snaps me out of my stupor.

It's a key being inserted into the front door handle.

Spencer is home.

CHAPTER 11
ABBY

Hurriedly I stuff the photos into my pockets, the crinkling of the paper making my heart pound as the front door swings open.

"Babe?"

"In here," I shout back, my voice coming out more strained than intended.

Like Katherine said, I can't reveal that I know the truth. Despite the evidence in my pocket, I need to remain as normal as I can.

Sweat seems to be seeping out of my pores as I make my way back into the living room, where Spencer is loosening the knot on his tie.

The image of him and some girl locked in a passionate embrace flashes across my mind, and my belly rolls.

He's smiling at me, but it doesn't warm my chest like it used to.

All I can see now are those heart-eye emojis he sent in response to photos of other women's bodies.

"Is everything okay? You look a little pale," Spencer says.

I blink, my mind scrambling. Should I confront him now, or continue to build my case?

"I'm... I think I might be coming down with something," I answer finally.

A severe case of cheating husband disease.

Spencer nods and gives me an empathetic look.

"Sorry to hear that. Might be allergies—it is spring, after all."

I manage a thin smile. "Could be."

"How was work?" I ask. The question comes out on a bit of a croak because my mouth is so dry.

I know he wasn't really at work this late, but I want to see what he says. Spencer opens the cabinet where we keep our drinking glasses but pauses to look back at me.

For a moment I actually think he's going to confess everything to me and fall on his knees, begging for my forgiveness.

Please don't.

As crushed as I am over what I've seen, I'm afraid part of me still loves him enough to forgive him if he asks.

But he doesn't. Instead, he rolls his eyes and blows out a huff of air.

"Just brutal. Looks like this whole week is going to be late nights."

His words hit me like a gut punch. He lies so easily to me it makes me nauseous. I swallow hard and smile again.

"Sorry to hear that."

Spencer shrugs and heads over to the fridge to pull out a bottle of beer. It splashes and foams in his glass as he pours it.

He looks up to find me watching him, though I quickly divert my eyes. I need to act normal, or he'll begin to think something is up.

I don't know what would happen then, and I can't even consider it just yet. Taking a small breath, I make my way to the couch and plop down.

All of the strength in my body seems to leak out onto the cushions beneath me.

Spencer lifts his glass and guzzles it, his Adam's apple moving up and down as he gulps down the booze.

A trickle of it drizzles down his chin and neck, the bead catching the light.

I'm staring again.

Hastily, I pull my attention away before he notices. I think I'm just trying to spot any outward signs of his infidelity—how could there be none?

How could I have completely missed this?

The pictures in my pocket feel like boulders pinning me down. My husband's emotional affairs.

Spencer comes around the kitchen island to make his way into the living room, a hand running across his mouth to mop up the errant droplets.

My heart slams against my ribs as he comes closer to me. His gaze is locked on my face.

A single thought flashes across my brain.

He knows.

All I can think about are the folded sheets of paper stuffed in my pocket. Somehow, he knows what I've been up to. Maybe he got a notification I'd logged in on his tablet.

The floorboards creak as he takes a couple steps closer to me, reducing the space between us to mere feet.

In the low lamplight, the shadows cast across his handsome face give it an almost sinister appearance.

He's still staring at me, a blank expression in his eyes.

"What?" I ask weakly.

He was the one who screwed up, so why do I feel so guilty?

Spencer doesn't respond, just comes to a stop beside the couch. He's still looking down at me. I swallow hard, my throat tight.

Then his hand comes up to feel my forehead, stilling me. He cups my head for a moment, adjusting his hand once before nodding.

"You do feel pretty warm. Maybe you are getting sick."

I nod, gulping. "Yeah. I'm gonna... I think I'm gonna go lie down."

"Good idea. I'll be in soon. I'm pretty beat myself."

I push off the couch arm and stand again, my heart rate spiking as the paper sheets in my pocket crinkle loudly.

Spencer looks down at me, a smile tugging at the corner of his lips as he notices my bulging pockets.

"What've you got stuffed in there?"

I blink hard, the breath suddenly having evaporated from my lungs. "Photos of me and Katherine from today. I... want to get into scrapbooking."

My words spill out, a little rambly but otherwise coherent enough that Spencer simply nods.

"Nice. Can I see? I still don't even know what Katherine looks like, despite her being your best friend. You two are like the only women I know who never take pictures."

Pictures. Girls in front of the mirror. Heart-eyes.

All of that rushes through my mind before I manage to digest Spencer's question, and then even more panic sets in. I can't let him look at the images I printed.

But what reason can I give for refusing him?

My head snaps back and forth in a blur. Spencer's eyebrows shoot up in surprise, so I quickly fire off another lie.

"I can show you later, when I've put it all together in the scrapbook. It's... it's not ready yet."

Spencer shrugs again as he falls back on the couch. "Okay."

I let out another puff of air, working to get my heartbeat back under control. I need to calm down, or Spencer will definitely begin to suspect something is amiss.

But how can I be calm, now that I know what I know?

It's impossible to go back to *normal*.

I make my way into the bedroom and shut the door

behind me, only allowing myself to breathe evenly once the door clicks shut.

I can just make out the hum of the TV in the other room as Spencer watches whatever sports talk show he's got on.

Leaning forward, I rest my forehead against the back of the door and shut my eyes. I can't be around Spencer for long, or he'll know something is wrong.

I'm just not that good at pretending.

I can't fake my marriage like he apparently can.

I haven't heard anything from Katherine since we parted ways at the bar, but that's to be expected.

Part of me doesn't want to hear anything from her at all, other than maybe that she looked into it, and everything my husband told me about his first wife checked out.

I'm honestly not sure I could handle anything more at this point.

For now, I need to hide these pictures somewhere safe. Somewhere Spencer won't think to look.

My eyes flash over the entirety of the bedroom. We keep a pretty minimalist aesthetic, which now means there aren't many good hiding places.

If I'd had more time before he came home, I could have put them somewhere there was no chance he'd ever find them.

Unfortunately, I have only a few minutes and only this bedroom and the adjoining bathroom to work with.

Then it hits me. A place no man would ever dream of checking.

I go into the bathroom as quietly as I can, my bare feet silent as I scurry to the door. It opens with a little squeak that freezes me again, but Spencer is too busy shouting at the TV to notice.

I step inside and zero in on my drawer in the vanity cabinet.

The folded sheets of paper crinkle some more as I pull

them out of my pocket, spiking my heart rate. Gently I open the drawer, revealing the box of tampons I've got stored in here.

Taking another breath, I remind myself that Spencer would have no reason to look in this box—and no reason to suspect me of anything. I've always loved him with my whole heart.

A tear slips down my cheek as that thought threatens to take me under.

I've loved him completely, and look where that got me.

The overhead light illuminates the printed images in my hands as I shakily insert them into the cardboard box.

The creased papers fit easily.

Once that's settled, I let out a long, shaking breath.

Then I go through my nightly routine like a zombie, drawing the toothbrush back and forth across my teeth as I stare blankly at myself in the mirror.

Distressing thoughts continue to swirl about my head, threatening to pull me under.

In the other room is a man who is not faithful to me. We occupy the same space and say *I love you* every day, and yet he does not belong to me in the same way I belong to him.

Another swell of nausea rocks me, and I have to grip tight to the marble countertop to avoid collapsing.

I finally manage to finish my routine then pad back to the bed and slip underneath the covers. It's pitch black in the bedroom, and warm beneath the heavyweight duvet.

I don't ever want to come out again.

As exhausted as I feel, and as much as I know I need to sleep, it doesn't come.

Within an hour Spencer quietly enters the bedroom and heads into the connected bathroom. For a moment worry has me in its grips—what if he finds the hidden pictures?

Then I hear him let out a cough and turn on the water. I force my pulse to settle.

Spencer exits the bathroom soon afterward, and I keep my eyes shut tightly, praying he can't hear the pounding of my heart in the darkness as he slips underneath the covers beside me.

He lets out another cough and then adjusts position. The mattress shifts and jiggles with his movements.

Soon enough he's asleep, leaving me to listen to the rhythmic sounds of his breathing in the darkness. I used to love to listen to his breathing.

There was something so comforting about it, knowing he was real and that he loved me. Now I can't stand it, because I know he breathes for someone else.

Someone younger, prettier. Tears sting the corners of my eyes and keep on coming, defeating my attempts to stop them. Eventually I'm forced to stuff my hand into my mouth to keep my sobs from waking Spencer up.

I silently cry until exhaustion finally begins to lull me into a shallow sleep.

And then just as I'm about to drift away, my phone buzzes.

It's a text from Katherine, and when I read it, any semblance of drowsiness disappears altogether.

Need to meet tomorrow—you need to see what I found.

CHAPTER 12
ABBY

The next morning passes in agonizing slowness.

After Katherine's late-night text, I was simply unable to fall asleep, my stomach roiling in anxiety over what she could've found out.

When daylight finally dawns, I'm utterly exhausted. The hangover doesn't help. At least it all supports the lie that I'm sick, so Spencer doesn't question my inability to get up and join him for breakfast in the kitchen.

He opens and closes the fridge, his footsteps clacking across the tile every so often as I lie in bed, feeling like I need to pee, run, and throw up at the same time.

I'm a total bundle of nerves that feels like it could explode at any moment.

I don't know if I have the strength to keep going. Katherine's text, combined with the truth about our relationship has me pinned under an anvil.

Eventually the bedroom door creaks open, but I don't react.

I can sense Spencer standing there a second before he shuts the door quietly again and then heads out of the apartment.

Only once I hear the sounds of him leaving and feel sure he's gone do I open my eyes.

There's absolutely no way I can eat breakfast right now, not with my stomach as nauseous as it is.

The apartment is eerily quiet.

Nothing has changed in my environment, and yet everything is different.

Before I never minded the silence—it had felt like a peaceful refuge from the busy city outside. Now, it just feels empty.

Devoid of love, trust, everything a marriage should consist of.

In this vacuous space, questions fill my mind. All of them shout to be heard.

Questions about my husband and what he's done.

There's no way I can just stay in this apartment all day with my thoughts and those printed pictures.

I'll lose my mind. Katherine is at work right now, which means there are multiple hours I need to fill before she can tell me what she found.

I know I need to work as well. I've hardly glanced at it since this nightmare began. There are only so many personal days a girl can take before people start to wonder, but nevertheless I'm not sure I have it in me today.

Still, I need to try, just so that the rest of my life doesn't crumble. I'll definitely need a job if I'm on my own.

The bell on the cafe door dings overhead as I step inside, my nose running from the brisk bite in the air. My eyes scan the counter—looks like Rachel is working today. Good. I could definitely use a friendly face.

The whole walk here, I was utterly consumed by Katherine's text.

Depending on what she found out, everything could change. Can I handle that?

Just the fact my husband was texting other women nearly destroyed me, and now there's this.

I take a shuddering breath and try to set my face in a way that looks like I'm not completely falling apart as I step into line.

Rachel smiles when I reach her.

"Morning, how are you?" she asks.

I manage to keep a smile on my face as I talk. "It's been a week, that's for sure."

"Good or bad?"

I know she's just asking to be polite, and I certainly don't want to dump all of my trauma on her in the line for a bagel. Instead, I shrug.

"Bit of both, I guess."

"Well, Rachel's having a great week—she *finally* met a guy," another girl behind the counter pipes up.

Rachel's cheeks color as she gives her co-worker a death stare before flicking her eyes back to me and shaking her head.

"I'm with a *customer*, Hannah. Go back on break."

I was too hungover to tell earlier, but the girl does seem to have a glow about her. How nice.

I should be congratulating her, because I can tell she's excited, but all I can think about is the man in my own life, and what he's done to me.

Part of me wants to grab Rachel by the shoulders and shake her to make sure she understands that men will break your heart without a second thought, but I don't.

"I'll do the usual, plus a large iced coffee," I say.

"Got it. I'll bring it over," Rachel says as she taps the screen in front of her.

She flashes Hannah another glare as I turn away from the counter, hearing Hannah breaking down into a fit of laughter behind me.

Oh, to be young and in love. That was me once.

With my order placed, I plop myself down into my regular seat with a huff and begin unloading my laptop from my bag.

Opening my email reveals a stomach-churning number of urgent messages that need my attention. At the very least, the sheer panic that my absence has caused might be enough to force me to focus on something other than my personal life, at least for the time being.

Two hours later, I decide it isn't.

Apparently all areas of my life are destined to suffer, because I can hardly concentrate for more than a couple seconds before Katherine's text rises up in my mind.

I check my phone again for what has to be the thousandth time, but as before, there is nothing. Katherine is still at work, just like she was two minutes ago.

Finally, after what seems like an eternity, the phone buzzes. It's Katherine, and she's calling me.

The phone is up by my ear in a flash, my heart in my throat.

"Hello?"

"Hey—can you hear me?" Katherine asks.

It sounds like she's at a concert. Must mean she's walking through the subway at lunchtime.

"Yeah, I can," I answer quickly.

My mouth has gone completely dry. I glance over at my drink, but it's long since been drained.

"So sorry about the cliffhanger, but there's too much to say just over text. Are you at home?" Katherine asks.

"I'm at Mud Pot," comes my reply.

"Okay, I guess that'll do," Katherine says, her voice sounding rushed as she moves through the crowd.

"So here it is—as soon as I got home, I started digging. Turns out, there's way less on this story than I could've ever imagined. It's almost like the police hardly even gave it a second look."

"But what I did find was that Shannon isn't missing

anymore. She's been officially declared dead—*literally this week*. Did Spencer mention any of this to you?"

"No," I say, "not a word."

"Apparently if a person is still missing after seven years, the courts declare them legally dead," Katherine continues, "which means no one has seen or heard from Shannon since literally the day she disappeared."

I can feel myself beginning to spiral. "That doesn't mean she's actually dead though," I say quickly.

"No hits on her credit card. Not a single sighting, Abby, not one. I looked through the police report on her case. The last time she was seen, she was heading toward the parking garage of her building on the day she disappeared."

"Spencer told me the building didn't have cameras in the parking garage, so police assumed she went out that way because she didn't want to be seen leaving the building," I throw out uselessly.

Everything feels like it's on fire. This can't be happening.

"I kept digging," Katherine says, undeterred. "Just because there wasn't much in the mainstream media about it doesn't mean nobody cares. There are these groups online, wholly dedicated to this sort of thing. I'm actually—never mind, it doesn't matter. But get this... someone actually dug up a security camera recording from the day she went missing. It's not from the streets around their apartment building, but it's not too far off."

I swallow hard, barely able to manage it around the huge lump in my throat. "And... what does it show?"

I have no more flimsy excuses or rebuttals to throw out. My eyes are shut tight as I prepare myself for what I know is about to come next.

"It's grainy, but legible. It shows a hooded figure dragging a blue suitcase. Rumor is Spencer had bought her a suitcase just like it. And Abby... the suitcase looks heavy."

CHAPTER 13
ABBY

My eyelids fly back open.

"Do they know who it is in the video?"

My heart is pounding, but this isn't the conclusive evidence I was expecting to hear.

"Like I said, the video is pretty poor quality. It was pulled off a food truck security camera positioned two blocks over, and the angle is kinda funky. So no, we don't know for sure," Katherine says over the phone.

"So it could be Shannon herself," I say.

"I admire your optimism," Katherine replies sarcastically.

I swallow hard. I must sound utterly ridiculous to her, defending Spencer as I am. I let out a sigh and rub my face.

"Abby, I know you love Spencer, and you think he told you the truth… but please, you can't possibly be this dumb."

Her words sting, jerking me upright in my seat as I blink. I know Katherine is a straight shooter, but that sounded straight up insulting.

"Excuse me for defending a man I have loved and lived with for five years," I say, surprised at how strong my voice sounds under the circumstances.

"Sorry, I'm sorry," Katherine replies instantly. "That was wrong of me. I'm sorry."

I let out a breath. Spencer is a slimy, unfaithful dirtbag, yes, but I don't think he's capable of something like that.

I think back to the first time Spencer told me about his first wife. We were on a date at a restaurant, and some man came up to Spencer wondering if he could ask him some questions.

I knew Spencer was no celebrity, and so I gave him a quizzical look. It took Spencer a moment, but eventually he told me about what had happened.

When he laid out the whole story—Shannon's disappearance, the police, the journalists, it all felt genuine.

I could tell he was exhausted from it all, and he offered the fatigue as the reason why he hadn't told me about it sooner.

People seem to look at me differently once they know, he said.

I asked him why he thought she left, and he responded that they had been having some marital issues up to that point. They weren't exactly on stellar ground, as he put it. So when he learned that she'd taken off, he wasn't entirely surprised.

Luckily, he had an alibi for the day she disappeared. He was working, completing a project. That was verified by a witness, and police released him.

When I heard all of that, looking him square in the face, I believed him. To me, it seemed entirely genuine.

Now however, I'm forced to wonder if maybe Spencer wasn't being so truthful about it all.

I pick up my coffee cup again, but it's still empty. My eyes flick over to the counter where Rachel and Hannah are both at their stations, tapping away madly at the screens in front of them as they take orders.

Then my gaze drifts up to the television in the corner.

The local news is on, and I see from the banner running across the bottom the news is still fixated on the story of Elizabeth Waters, the murdered girl found in the park.

That's not what holds my attention, though. What grabs me are the images of the girl's apartment that just flashed across the screen.

An apartment I could swear I've seen before.

"Abby?"

I blink, my attention pulled from the crime scene photo and recentered on the phone in my hand.

"Sorry, I… Katherine, I need to call you back," I stammer.

My eyes remain glued to the television.

The still images showing the girl's apartment are police photos, which indicates to me that they suspect the killer was in her apartment at some point.

They flash the photograph of the apartment bathroom again, the one that caught my attention. It looks like any other tiny New York City apartment bathroom, apart from the white and blue checkered shower curtain.

That's what I recognized—that distinctive pattern and color. I swear I've seen it before, but where?

Then it hits me. The dating app pictures on Spencer's phone.

At least, I think that's where I saw it. I need to get back home *right now* and make sure.

All I can think about is that distinctive white and blue checker pattern as I hustle down the sidewalk, my breath coming in short gulps.

Was it the same pattern?

I rack my brain to try and conjure up the image, but I can't see it clearly. It's maddening, like an itch I can't seem to scratch, but I *know* I've seen that curtain before.

I need to get home.

Moving as quickly as I can, I pass between the other pedestrians who walk with their coats buttoned and shoulders hunched. The tightness in my stomach keeps the chill at bay.

My legs begin to burn as I go, but my eyes remain glued

on our apartment building in the distance. The truth is in there, up in our bathroom.

Part of me clings to hope that I'm misremembering what I saw, that maybe the pattern is a different one, or a lighter shade of blue.

The other part of me, the part that makes my body feel like it weighs a thousand pounds, reminds me how much I truly don't know about my husband. Especially after this week.

Could he actually have slept with a girl who was murdered shortly afterward?

And if he did, that begs another question.

Did my husband have something to do with her death?

I arrive at our building in record time, and then I'm racing toward the elevator, barely giving a nod to a neighbor before I slip inside.

As the doors open on our floor, the padded carpet beneath my feet obscures the sounds of my footsteps as I race back toward our apartment.

My hands shake as I fish out our key from my pocket, and the small piece of metal glances off the keyhole a couple of times before it finally sinks into place.

The apartment is just as I left it, but I hardly pay attention as I shoot to the bedroom and then the bathroom.

At the vanity I yank open the drawer and rip open the box of tampons.

Here they are, the images.

I flip through the pages as fast as I can.

Where is it? I know I've seen that pattern, and I really think I recognized it from one of—

My entire body freezes solid as I come across a flash of checkered blue.

The bathroom shown in this picture is an *exact match* for the one on the television in the café.

CHAPTER 14
ABBY

I can hardly breathe.

My eyes dart back and forth, taking in every detail of the picture in my hands, looking for any inconsistency.

I race back out into the living room and turn on the TV, locating the same channel that was playing in the café.

It's a morning talk and news show, and they're still discussing Elizabeth Waters and the latest developments in her case.

My eyes scan the headline at the bottom of the screen, reading that police suspect she was killed by a secret lover.

The words send a pang of fear through my heart.

My husband was one of this girl's secret lovers.

But there's no way he could've had something to do with her murder... could he?

A week ago, I would've dismissed any idea like that as absolute lunacy, but the revelations I've had over the past few days have me questioning everything.

I truly don't know my husband as I thought I did. Is he capable of such a horrific act against a young woman?

Cheating on me is one thing. Cheating on me and then killing the girl he cheated with is another thing entirely.

HIS FIRST WIFE 85

I remain fixated on the screen, hoping they'll show the image of Elizabeth's bathroom again so I can compare it to the picture in my hand.

I can still see the patterned shower curtain in my head, and it exactly matches the one in my photo.

When I first saw this image, I didn't even think about the background. Not when there was a young woman's naked body taking up most of the frame.

But somewhere in my subconscious, it must have stuck. I run my eyes over the photo again.

Scattered along the countertop in front of the young woman are various creams and lotions, stacked in a rather hectic way.

The photograph carousel begins on the news again, flashing images of the park, caution tape, and a shot of Elizabeth's living room.

Then, the bathroom. I pause the television on the bathroom image. It's frozen on my screen, blown up much larger than it was on the café TV.

With the larger size, there's no mistaking it.

It's an identical layout. Even down to the various lotions and creams, many of which are in the same positions as they are in the photo she sent my husband.

I sift rapidly through the rest of the paper pile to find their conversation.

My hands go numb as I spot the name at the top of their message thread.

Liz. Oh no, this is definitely the same girl.

When was the photo sent to Spencer?

Another thunderclap. The time stamp shows it was sent just over a week ago.

That means that mere days after sending this picture to my husband, Elizabeth Waters would be found dead in Central Park.

My hands are shaking so hard now that it makes the paper

flap around.

I slowly lower myself to the couch before I pass out. I feel lightheaded.

I'm blinking hard, trying to make my fractured mind understand what this could possibly mean.

Is it just the world's worst coincidence? Or something more sinister?

Even with my eternal optimism where he's concerned, I'm having trouble coming up with an explanation that doesn't point to my husband as a murderer.

But how could I have lived with the man for five years without having a clue?

I don't know what to believe anymore. I pull out my phone and tap on Katherine's name so I can explain why I hung up on her so abruptly.

She answers immediately. "Abby, are you okay? You sounded really weird when—"

"Spencer was texting her," I interrupt. "The girl they found in the park, Spencer was texting her."

The words hang in the air. One second. Two.

"*What*?" Katherine gasps.

I nod and raise my hand clutching the proof, though of course Katherine can't see it.

"I've got it right here. One of the photos I screenshotted. It was taken in the same bathroom they just showed on the news."

"He knew her, Katherine," I finish, breathless.

She says something in response, but I can't make it out. My heartbeat is whirring loudly in my ears as I think back to when Spencer and I first turned on the news and saw the story on Elizabeth.

What a shame. That's all he said.

A girl he was texting with, sending half-naked photographs back and forth with. He learned she was dead, and all he had to say was *what a shame*.

Could he truly be that callous?

"Do the screenshots show anything about them meeting up?" Katherine asks.

Her questions pull me back to reality, and I scramble to sift through the papers once again, searching to find the conclusion of their messaging.

After a moment, I shake my head. "No. It ends with Spencer writing, *Daddy needs to see that sexy body in person*, but there's nothing after that."

How quickly things have changed.

That revolting statement from my husband to a woman who isn't me hardly makes a dent in my psyche now, considering these new revelations.

"Still, I think we need to go to the police—they need to hear about this," Katherine says.

It's a total escalation, but this time I don't disagree with her.

———

It takes longer than I expected to speak with someone at the station. Though we told the person at the front desk it might be a matter of life and death, Katherine and I have been sitting in this dingy waiting room for nearly twenty minutes.

Katherine glances at her watch then shakes her head.

"We're holding information about the most highly publicized murder in years, and they're going to make me late getting back to work," she says.

Finally, a door creaks open.

"This way, please," a man says before turning and heading down a hallway.

Katherine and I glance at each other then get up and follow him. The officer stops in front of the door of what I can only assume is an interrogation room and gestures for us to enter.

It's cold inside. There's a single metal table in the center, and the single window high in the corner is so tiny a cat couldn't fit through it.

"Nice place," Katherine remarks as she does a slow spin, surveying the space.

The man starts to head out, pausing for a moment with his hand on the door.

"Won't be long. We appreciate your patience."

Then we're alone again. There's nothing to do but sit, so we sit.

Another wait. This time, almost ten minutes.

When the door finally opens again, a man and a woman step inside, talking among themselves.

I straighten in my chair, but the two detectives haven't even acknowledged us yet.

"And that's only *one* of them," the man says with a pointed look at his companion, seemingly ending whatever conversation the two had going.

"Afternoon," the man says to us.

He drops a notebook on the table and adjusts his pants before taking a seat with a heavy sigh. The woman follows suit.

I lean forward, eager to start talking, but the man starts before I can open my mouth.

"I'm Detective Sullivan, this is Detective Marsh. I understand you may have possible information regarding the Elizabeth Waters case?"

I nod. The woman glances between Katherine and me but doesn't say a word.

"Her husband," Katherine bursts out, "he was texting with her. Like, sending pictures."

I produce the printed sheets, which make both officers lean forward. I expect wide eyes, gasps, maybe even a heartfelt thank you.

Instead, Detective Sullivan scans the printouts for less than ten seconds then lets out a sigh. He passes the papers to Marsh, who doesn't sigh, but doesn't look exactly interested either.

"What?" Katherine asks.

"Ms..." Detective Sullivan begins.

Katherine crosses her arms. "May. Katherine May."

"Ms. May, we appreciate you coming in. Both of you."

"But?" Katherine asks.

Detective Sullivan glances over at Detective Marsh, who remains completely impassive.

"There's nothing here," he says.

My eyebrows furrow. "Nothing there? That's my husband *flirting* with a girl who was then found *murdered*."

Sullivan tongues a molar as he nods. "And I'm sorry about that. Thing is, this isn't anything new. We've been through Ms. Waters's phone, all her conversations."

Katherine stares. "And?"

Another look at Detective Marsh before speaking. "And... there are over two dozen similar conversations with men held over the past few months, some of which included an actual meet up. We crossed Spencer Stevens off the list of possibles days ago."

I blink, unsure what to feel.

Relief? Disappointment?

Katherine doesn't seem satisfied either. She scoffs.

"You do know about Spencer, right? I mean, his history?" she asks.

Detective Sullivan gives another nod, but he's leaning back in his chair now, disengaged.

"We are aware. Mr. Stevens was released without suspicion regarding the disappearance of Mrs. Stevens seven years ago."

"Well, have you seen this?" Katherine asks.

Her phone lands on the tabletop. On it is the grainy

footage from the food truck camera. Katherine taps the screen.

"A hooded figure dragging a heavy blue suitcase bearing remarkable similarities to the one Spencer was said to have purchased for Shannon just days before her disappearance."

Detective Sullivan takes a second to move, but eventually he pushes himself forward to view the video properly. I study his face and see little change in emotion.

"When was this?" he asks.

"That video was taken the *day* she went missing," Katherine says.

"Would you mind if we made a copy of that, for our records?" Sullivan asks, his eyes flicking up to Katherine's face.

She shakes her head, clearly aggravated. "What more do you guys need, a smoking gun? That's Spencer on tape, dragging a suitcase with his wife inside it."

At that, Detective Marsh raises a hand. Detective Sullivan picks up Katherine's phone and hands it to her. She watches the video and then puts the phone back on the table.

"You don't agree?" Katherine asks, crossing her arms.

"Can't be. Stevens was at work, that's been confirmed. Maybe that's Shannon herself," Detective Sullivan replies.

Katherine looks over at me, her mouth open. I don't know what to think. I don't know what I *want* to think.

"Mrs. Stevens wanted to run away. Would make sense she wears a hood so she isn't recognized," Sullivan says.

Katherine's disgruntled face turns back to him. "And the heavy suitcase?"

"She packed up her life and left home. Of course the suitcase is gonna be heavy. Ask me, you found proof of Shannon being alive, not the opposite."

Katherine scoffs again, but this time doesn't argue.

Sullivan gathers up his notebook and my printed proof of Spencer's conversations.

"We'll go ahead and keep these for our records. Thank you for coming down to the station. The New York Police Department appreciates your willingness to aid us in the case."

His words have a certain rehearsed tone to them that tells me neither detective really appreciates it at all. To them, we're just another dead end.

Back outside, Katherine releases a long sigh as she rubs her forehead. Quickly though, she turns to me and apologizes.

"I'm sorry. Maybe you're right. Maybe the police are right, too. I just... I can't help feeling like we're all missing something here."

People pass us on the sidewalk, moving quickly to get wherever they need to go. Katherine rubs her hands together and eyes me.

"I know he's your husband, but I don't trust him, Abby."

I chew my lip. "I guess I can't trust him anymore either."

Katherine starts to nod, only to reach out and grab my arm at a speed that makes me jump.

"Follow him," she says.

My eyes bulge. I did say I wanted the truth, as hard as it might be to handle, but I'm no detective.

Apparently sensing my apprehension, she adds, "They just declared Shannon *dead*, Abby."

"Okay," I say. "I'll do it."

The idea has injected me with a sense of adrenaline I didn't possess just a few minutes ago. Taking such a bold step would've been unheard of for me prior to this week. I don't know who this new Abby is, but I don't mind it.

I nod to Katherine, my mind beginning to spin. "Spencer did say this whole week he was going to have to work late."

"Perfect—you can catch him in a lie," she says.

After the past few days of confusion, I feel a comforting sense of direction. I'll start today, head over to the building where Spencer works and follow him to see where he goes when he leaves.

If he is cheating, I'll have further proof of his infidelity.

More than that, I really want to see how he behaves when he's not around me.

In the messages I read, he seemed almost like an entirely different person.

I can't imagine the Spencer I know killing Elizabeth Waters, but this stranger on the apps? Who knows?

It's decided. I'll follow him tonight, watch and see what he does, where he goes, and with whom.

With this plan in mind, I feel a little bit better for the first time since getting that mysterious note. This is a chance for me to regain some of the control I lost when all this came to light.

Time to see what my husband's been up to.

By the time I get over to Spencer's building, the sun has already moved across the sky and sunk behind the high rises.

What light remains paints the city in a weak yellow glow. Within a few hours, darkness will descend.

Across from Spencer's work building is one of those healthy, fast casual restaurants. I go inside and order a tasteless salad even though I'm not hungry. I need to kill some time, and the place offers a good vantage point.

When he leaves, I'll be able to see him go.

It's still relatively early in the afternoon, so there's definitely going to be a bit of a wait. Once I get my salad, I settle into a counter seat facing the window.

I can see the main door of his building clearly from here. There's no way I'll miss him when he leaves.

Every so often the door opens, snapping me to attention. Each time it isn't him. Once the clock hits five-thirty, a steadier stream of people begins to filter out of the office building.

According to Spencer, that's when most of the support

staff goes home. Apparently, upper management types like him usually have to work later.

At this point, though, I'm not sure I believe that story anymore.

Regardless, I haven't seen him. By six-thirty, I'm beginning to wonder if he's even at work at all.

The door to my restaurant opens, letting in the loud voices of three men wearing vests and dress shirts.

The distraction pulls me away from my stakeout for just a moment.

As I return to my across-the-street vigil, I catch the back of a dark head of hair. The man just stepped out of Spencer's building and turned down the sidewalk.

This time, I know who it is.

Spencer, and he's on the move.

CHAPTER 15
SPENCER

It's been a tough week, and I could hardly wait to get out of work today.

Some reporter called me *at my office* to ask if I wanted to comment on the news about Shannon being declared officially dead.

Oh sure, I'd just love that chat about that... idiot.

Naturally, I didn't take the call, but it came in initially to one of the secretarial pool. Which means word got around the office within minutes. It was just like seven years ago all over again.

No one said anything to my face, but I could tell by the way they all looked at me. Definitely a flashback moment, and not a good one. The judgement was so intense back then, I nearly quit my job.

Now I'm glad I didn't. I've got a good thing going here, making a lot of money, working with Jane—taking long lunches with Jane.

Maybe this'll all blow over.

It's been seven years, after all, and I know how the media works. It won't be long until something new comes along and pulls their attention away.

At least I'll get a chance to blow off some steam tonight. I'm finally going to meet up with New Girl.

A perfect antidote to a stressful week.

Our schedules have finally aligned, and it couldn't have come at a better time.

As I strut down the sidewalk to meet her, I can only hope that she won't ask me about the case too. It's always so awkward when I try to explain my side to someone new.

They never seem to believe me. Except Abby, bless her heart.

Maybe part of that is my own doing, if I'm being completely honest. I mean, I wasn't *entirely* truthful about the whole situation. I wasn't actually at work, like I told the police.

I knew how bad it looked, so I came up with the idea to have Jane corroborate the story.

The cops were definitely suspicious, but with Jane backing me up, what could they say?

They bought it and eventually cleared me.

Thinking back on it, that was probably the first evidence that Jane was into me.

She had to have been, considering I asked her to lie to the police, no questions asked. I still can't believe she did it and never asked what I'd been up to instead of working on the project with her, like she said I was.

It's a good thing she didn't ask, because I could never tell her the truth.

A brisk wind billows between the buildings, riding up underneath my coat and sending a chill up my back. I can't wait for it to be warm again. Having to bundle up so much prevents everyone from seeing the incredible shape I've worked so hard to get myself in.

At least tonight, there's a good chance one girl will get to see.

That puts a smile on my face and some pep in my step. I

pick up my pace, deftly passing slower walkers on the sidewalk before crossing the street after a taxi flashes by.

I told her I'd be there soon, but I'm going to be a few minutes late.

It's a special move of mine, something of a trademark.

Shows the girl I'm meeting she's not all that important to me, which in turn makes her want me even more. Simple human psychology, courtesy of Dr. DeLuca.

Not sure why he'd offer that tidbit up, given he was basically condoning marital infidelity, but I certainly didn't mind. It's worked like a charm so far.

A horn honks to my right, drawing my attention. Some fool on a bike nearly got clipped weaving between cars at a green light. I shake my head and keep moving, sucking in a short, cold breath.

I've got to put all that Shannon stuff out of mind. It definitely won't enhance my charisma to be thinking of my dead first wife while on a date, that's for sure.

It takes longer than I'd like to sort myself out, but by the next block all of those thoughts are gone.

I've always prided myself on being able to compartmentalize. That's probably how I'm able to get away with cheating so easily.

An odd feeling comes over me as I stand at the next corner, waiting for the crosswalk light to turn. It disrupts my mojo a little. Turning side to side, I glance around the street, but I see nothing out of the ordinary.

Strange. Felt like I was being watched for a second there, but it's gone now.

Probably just my guilty conscience at play.

I've always thought the best remedy for a guilty conscience is a distraction, and I'm always on the lookout for a new one.

Because I've certainly got plenty to be guilty about.

CHAPTER 16
SHANNON
SEVEN YEARS AGO

I don't know how to act around him anymore.

Right now, Spencer is sitting there on the couch in the other room, scrolling on his phone while a football game plays loudly on the TV.

Other than the bandage over his cut, there's no evidence of the madman he turned into that night, nothing about his demeanor that resembles that terrifying creature he became.

Still, I don't feel right. About him. About us.

I don't think I ever will again.

Spencer seems to be under the impression that all is forgiven, that I took his infidelity in stride and have moved on. Only the days have, not my feelings.

At first, I was angry. Now I'm afraid.

Afraid of what he might do to me, what he's capable of.

Spencer shouts at the television as something happens in the game, jarring me enough that I jump a little on the mattress.

The past week has been a blur.

Days and nights spent going through the motions during the daytime and lying there at night, trapped in my own mind, screaming silently as Spencer hugs me, kisses me, lies beside me.

After the shock of his sudden outburst receded, a sinking feeling set in. It grows deeper whenever I recall what he said.

I can't handle a divorce. Promise you won't divorce me... I don't know what I'd do.

It was the tone with which he said it that chilled me to the bone. That voice told me that for whatever reason, my husband would do anything to avoid being left.

Anything.

Pushing myself off the bed, I take in a weary breath and rub my face. I haven't been sleeping well since it happened, and it shows. Spencer probably would've made a comment about my eye bags, except that he's not an idiot and doesn't want to push his perceived luck.

For now, it's good that he thinks all is forgiven.

If he doesn't suspect I'm planning to leave him, it'll be a little easier to pull off. I have to be careful. He's made it clear he doesn't want to lose me, and now he's demonstrated what he'll do if he doesn't get his way.

I step into the bathroom and turn on the sink. The water pouring from the faucet draws me in, cascading down and pooling in the—

"Everything okay?"

Spencer. I blink and look to the left, finding my husband leaning against the doorframe, watching me.

He's much taller than I am and fills out most of the doorway. Standing there as he is, he's got me completely boxed in our small bathroom.

I swallow the sudden claustrophobia and manage a smile. "Sorry. Still groggy from that nap."

Spencer continues to watch me, his eyes moving slowly over my face. The intensity of his gaze makes my skin grow hotter, like I'm under a magnifying glass in the sun.

He doesn't stop staring either, even when excited shouts from the television sound through the apartment.

"You're not still mad at me, are you?" he asks in a soft voice.

His eyes begin to well up with tears, making my heart beat faster. This man has weaponized emotions.

Hurriedly I shake my head, not wanting to witness another tantrum. Maybe he'd cry, maybe he'd do something worse this time.

Something about Spencer seems to settle, his shoulders lowering a couple inches.

"Good," he says, "you have nothing to worry about, okay? I messed up, and I take full responsibility for that."

As you should. You're the one who cheated, not me.

"I just… I don't want to lose you," he continues, "the hurt would be too much—not to mention all the other problems it would cause, for both of us."

As the words waft toward me, I finally understand. It's not me in particular that he cares about. It's the idea of us, our relationship as man and wife.

It's not that he wants to stay together because he loves me.

He doesn't want to split the apartment, or the bank account, or have to explain at every work function why his wife left him.

As realization dawns, I feel a cold shudder work its way through my body. I manage to obscure it with a reach toward the hand towel.

Spencer takes a step into the bathroom, filling the space with his presence. I fight hard not to shy away from him. He disgusts me in every way, but I have to keep up appearances.

He pulls me into a hug, wrapping one hand around my head and pressing it to his chest.

"I love you, you know," he says in a low voice, "I don't want us to have any problems."

His words reverberate in his chest, filtering through his

shirt before reaching my ears. I used to adore being held by him like this, but now I can't stand it.

I feel like I'm going to fly apart if he doesn't let me go soon.

Gently Spencer strokes the back of my head. It's the total opposite to his outburst, but it doesn't comfort me.

I'm too occupied with a singular question that won't stop pounding across my mind.

I'm beginning to wonder if my husband would harm me to keep me from leaving him.

CHAPTER 17
ABBY

Spencer is ahead of me—somewhere.

He headed down the sidewalk so fast after leaving the building, and it took me a minute to cross the street and follow him. Now I've lost track of him in the crowd.

The sidewalk is thick with pedestrians, what with it being after work and all. It makes my search for Spencer all the more challenging.

Where did he go?

Just a second ago I had him. His navy blue suit was easy to pick out, though now mixed with the rest of the horde, I've apparently lost him.

He blends easily with the army of businessmen and their boardroom haircuts.

Biting my lip, I cast my gaze ahead, searching the gaps in the crowd between us for any sign of him.

My heart squeezes in my chest at the idea of losing Spencer without gaining any new information. I need to know.

There—he just came into view when he made a right turn

at the corner. I shoot down the sidewalk after him, heart pounding and nerves on fire as I follow.

He's moving with purpose, like there's something he's eager to get to. Or someone. This is no ambling stroll.

Swallowing hard, I duck around a couple walking arm-in-arm, trying to keep up with Spencer's pace. He has longer legs than me, so he's able to cover more distance at a faster pace than I am.

I'm practically jogging to catch up to him as I finally reach the corner and turn right as he did.

The sidewalk ahead is cast in dark shadow and much less populated than the previous street. There's Spencer, about three-quarters of the way down the block already.

If he were to turn around right now, he'd spot me in an instant.

Hurriedly I cross to the other side of the street and tug the corners of my jacket up so that they obscure parts of my face. With my beanie covering my hair, I don't think he'd recognize me.

It's much colder here in the shade, and my body shivers, though I'm walking fast in an effort to keep pace with my husband.

At the end of the sidewalk, he pauses only a moment before crossing between cars. Traffic is stopped by a red light, though by the time I reach the intersection it's turned green again.

I have to wait for the next few cars to pass, my heart in my throat. Spencer is already moving quickly down the sidewalk across the way, and for a moment I lose sight of him between groups of people.

Finally he emerges again, just as a break in the traffic allows me to shoot across the street. A pothole in the cracked pavement is filled with dirty rainwater that ripples as I leap over it and start jogging after Spencer again.

The people around me seem to be walking impossibly

slowly, making my heart pound even faster as I squeeze between them.

"Sorry," I mutter as my shoulder jostles a woman wearing a heavy fur coat.

"Watch it," she hisses from behind me, but I don't turn around.

Spencer is at the next crosswalk, head tilted down to look at his watch before he's walking again. I pick up my pace, my thighs burning. I don't slow down.

He's less than twenty feet in front of me now as I suck rapid breaths of cold, sharp air into my lungs. The crosswalk sign flashes an orange hand that tells me not to cross, but I do it anyway so as not to lose sight of Spencer again.

A car honks, jarring me but not shaking me off course. Finally, I'm across and looking for Spencer.

He's about halfway down the block, but he's moved to the other side of the street. We must be getting close now to whatever his destination is.

I cross too, eyes locked on his back as he moves swiftly. This area of the street is much quieter, so much so that I can hear my own hurried footsteps echo off the buildings around me.

Hopefully it's not so loud that Spencer hears them as well and turns around to investigate. I slow for a moment. He's paused at the next corner, waiting for the light to turn.

Then he turns to glance back over his shoulder—turning toward me.

I see the side of his face as he twists, my stomach going watery at the realization that I have nowhere to hide.

He's going to see me—I'm going to get caught following him, and then who knows what will happen.

CHAPTER 18
ABBY

Desperately I jerk my head down, staring hard at the concrete beneath my feet as the seconds pass with a pulsing count in my head.

One. Did he recognize me?

Two. If he did, this game is over.

Three. Why hasn't he said anything?

My throat is so tight I can hardly swallow, but slowly I bring my head back up.

Spencer is no longer looking back in this direction. Instead, he's crossing the street as if nothing happened.

He didn't see me—or if he did, he didn't recognize me. I let out a breath, my hands trembling inside my jacket pockets as I take a few unsteady steps in his direction.

Across the street, Spencer stops in front of a warmly lit bar.

A welcoming orange glow pours out of large antique windows framed in black-painted wooden trim.

He lifts a hand to someone I can't see behind the glass and then tugs on the door before disappearing inside. The door shuts behind him, leaving me alone on the street.

I chew my lip and then cross the street again so I'll be on

the opposite side from the bar. There's scaffolding on the corner. The thick metal poles will serve as cover.

That way, if Spencer were to look out, he'd have a harder time spotting me.

Time seems to slow as I reach the crosswalk, my gaze locked on the bar's amber glow up and to my right. From here I can just make out a few tables pushed up against the windows.

Behind them there are a few people seated at the bartop itself.

Each step across the asphalt echoes louder in my mind as I draw closer. Suddenly my feet feel like they weigh a hundred pounds each.

What will I see when I get close enough for a good look inside?

Who is Spencer there to meet?

I reach the sidewalk on the other side of the street and step under the scaffolding. My chest is so tight I can hardly breathe.

This is it. After the photos, after the news reports, after everything... I've become a woman who stalks her husband. Taking a deep breath, I ease a little farther down so that I've got a view between the poles into the bar windows across the street.

Even though the place is pretty empty, it takes me a moment to spot Spencer.

Once I do, I wish I hadn't.

He's seated at a table against the bar's back wall. Beside him—or I should say, intertwined with him—is a woman.

A younger woman.

Though I can't see her face, I can tell her age by the clothing she's wearing. Her jeans are wide legged in a way that's fashionable with women under thirty.

A dark puffy coat with a white faux fur hood adorns the top half of her. So chic.

With her back angled toward the window, I can't get a clear view of her face.

She must've said something hilarious though because Spencer erupts into a fit of laughter, his hand slapping the tabletop as his head angles back.

Seeing that hurts the most somehow.

I thought he only laughed like that with me. I bite my lip, mentally forcing myself to keep watching even as tears threaten to stream down my face.

Reaching out, I grip onto a freezing scaffolding support beam. The sharp temperature of the metal grounds me enough to continue.

Spencer leans forward, as does the woman. Then they kiss, and finally, there's no mistaking it.

My husband is unfaithful to me—emotionally and physically. I've seen it with my own eyes.

This is confirmation that it's more than just emotional cheating or sending flirty messages. Here he is, in the flesh, meeting another woman and kissing her and laughing with her like he used to do with me.

I feel very much like I've been shot in the heart.

Seeing the way he holds her hands, lazily intertwining his fingers with hers… it's the exact same thing he does with me.

That crushes my spirit even more as I stagger backward into the wall behind me and use it for support. I'm afraid if I'm not leaning against something, my legs will simply give out from beneath me, and I'll drop in a puddle to the ground.

All my worst fears come crashing down on me as it truly sets in that my husband is a cheater.

Another thought hits me in between the sobs that swell up and threaten to swamp me. Katherine would want me to get photos of this.

As my chest heaves, I manage to pull my phone out of my pocket and hold it up in a shaky hand. Tears swim in my eyes and blur my vision, making the task near impossible.

Somehow, I manage to switch my phone over to the camera app, using my fingers to zoom in roughly so I can take photos of the two of them holding hands at the back of the bar.

Though the images come out slightly blurry, you can still tell it's Spencer because of the watch he wears on his left hand.

It's his favorite watch, and he never goes anywhere without it.

It has a distinctive yellow and blue striped band that he's worn since I've known him.

The girl's arm is raised in the photo too, her stupid fluffy fur hood bending with her movement. I stare down at the photo for another second, my stomach tightening until I'm about to vomit and have to look away.

I can't stand here much longer, or I don't know what's going to happen.

And I don't have to stay and watch this any longer. I have the evidence now, and the proof tells me the full truth. I turn and begin walking back toward our apartment in a daze.

The world continues to operate around me as usual, though none of it seems real. It all feels like some sort of play production, a bunch of background actors going through the motions as I stumble forward, reeking of misery.

I nearly miss the stop-walking sign, and I'm only saved from stepping into traffic by a shrill horn that snaps me back to reality. A speeding taxi flies past, inches away.

All I can see in my head is Spencer and the woman holding hands in the bar.

Sitting there like two lovers without a care in the world.

Tears threaten to spill over again, but I manage to keep them down until I get back to my building.

In the lobby, I manage a weak smile for a delivery driver who barely looks up at me before I turn away and scurry over to the elevators.

Only once the elevator doors shut do I let the tears flow, feeling a potent mixture of anger and sadness crash over me all at once. It's a terrible storm that I have no hope of controlling.

Spencer isn't the man I knew, nor is he the man I thought I married. When I made the decision to marry him, I took our vow seriously.

We swore to each other that we would be there until the very end, just us two.

He's broken that vow now, and I don't know what to do.

I can't imagine being with another man or having to go out there and date again. I thought I was through with all that forever.

I have to lean against the side of the elevator for support, taking hitching breaths until it dings to signal I've reached my floor.

When the door slides open, I shoot out of it, but it's no better in the hallway. I feel like the walls are closing in around me.

Inside our apartment, it's all I can do to make it to the bed where I collapse and cry into the pillow.

It all pours out of me in a tidal wave of emotion, a mix of sobs and screams that are absorbed by the plush blankets and pillows and crisp white sheets, now damp with my tears.

My picture-perfect life has officially been completely, utterly destroyed.

CHAPTER 19
ABBY

Some distant part of me becomes aware that the phone is ringing, though I don't know for how long.

Slowly I drag my head up and blink, looking around as I try to figure out what time it is. My phone is lying upside down on the floor, buzzing against the rug beside my bed.

Without leaving the safety of the covers, I stick out a hand and scoop up the phone. The blazing brightness of the screen makes me squint as I look to see who's calling me.

It's Katherine. No doubt she wants to know what became of my stakeout, but I'm not sure I can talk about it right now.

I don't think I can talk to anyone.

Even though I know she'll be sympathetic, there will also be a sense of *I told you so* that I'm just not ready for yet.

I feel raw and utterly broken, and there's no one in the world who could console me right now.

Knowing she'll grow concerned if she doesn't hear from me though, I pull myself together enough to fire off a short text.

Saw him with some girl.

Then I turn my phone off and collapse into the sheets once again.

It's another thirty minutes or so before finally I feel like I've cried all I can cry, and I sit stiffly on the edge of the bed, the tips of my toes touching the carpet.

I'm numb. I could literally get shot, and I don't think I'd feel a thing.

It's late now, nearly midnight. Spencer still hasn't come home.

That makes my stomach turn all over again.

What, does he really think I'll believe he had to stay at the office that late? He must think I'm stupid.

Tomorrow morning I'll confront him about everything, showing him the proof I have.

It won't feel good, but I know it's what I've got to do.

Tonight though, I just can't handle it.

Lying in bed, I stare blankly at the wall and windows in front of me. I hardly even blink, the minutes and then hours passing in total silence. Still no sign of my husband.

I'm beyond tears at this point. There's nothing left of me.

At some point during the wee hours of morning, the front door opens with a small squeak. Spencer has finally returned.

I remain on my side with my back to the bedroom door. I hear him padding around the kitchen for a few minutes before he enters the bedroom. The door opens, and a ray of light is cast across the bed.

I shut my eyes and try to keep my breathing as even as possible as I hear Spencer cross the room and enter the bathroom.

The hiss of the shower hits my ears. Washing off whatever sins he's committed, no doubt.

My thoughts race as I lie there, wondering if I should say something right now, but I quickly think better of it.

I'm in too fragile of an emotional state and just feel too raw to deal with it.

When Spencer finishes up in the bathroom, I hear the door open and then he softly creeps over to his side of the bed and climbs in with me.

I feel my body stiffen as he lets out a grunt and shifts around. The mattress shifts beneath me with his movement, but I remain still. He's less than a few feet from me now physically. Mentally, we're a thousand miles apart.

Tears form again as I picture him holding hands with that girl.

I hate that part of me still wants to roll over and hug him as I would've done in the past when he'd come to bed after a long workday, to claim him as mine.

That pitiful part of me still aches for the intimacy that I know that we had at one point.

Is it truly gone forever?

Spencer clearly seems to think so.

I don't know what happened with us. How did we get to this point?

I feel like I'm at war with myself, part of me wanting to look past this because I love him so much, and the other part hating him for what he's done and how he's making me feel.

What's even worse is that he seems to feel no guilt whatsoever, as he lies there beside me. I can hear the flipping of pages as he reads a chapter from the book he's working through.

It's his normal nightly routine, but it feels almost mocking now after what I've seen.

I feel entirely on edge as if at any moment, Spencer will tap me on the shoulder and ask why I was watching him earlier.

I bite my lip as I stare blankly out the dark window across the room, my eyes drawn to the single glowing square in the apartment building across the street.

There's no movement.

The light doesn't reveal much more than a lamp just

inside the glass. I wonder who lives there, whose life is happening so close to mine. I wonder if they'd care how much of a wreck my life has become.

Daylight has begun to filter across the horizon by the time I finally manage to pass out.

When I wake up again, Spencer is already in the bathroom getting ready for work.

I crack an eyelid open, cringing from the pounding headache battering my skull.

I must've gotten less than an hour of sleep last night, and my body is definitely expressing its disapproval.

I don't know how I'll be able to face Spencer in such a state, but I know I have to. My eyes shift to the clock and then blink. It's barely seven. He's up earlier than usual.

Most of the city isn't even awake yet, judging by the silence of the normally noisy street below.

I flick my eyes up toward the window I saw last night, but it's dark now.

Then I look at the bathroom door, which is still shut. The shower is running again.

Why is Spencer getting ready already? Does he suspect something is going on? Does he know that I know?

My heart begins to pound, pulsing in rhythm with the headache as I shift upright in the bed.

I reach for my phone and groan at the sudden blast of brightness when it turns on.

There is a string of texts from Katherine, which is strange. She doesn't usually text me this early in the morning.

I hear the water shut off behind me as I let out a shuddering yawn and tap on the messages to see what Katherine has to say.

"That girl you saw him with… what did she look like???" reads the first text.

Then, *"When did Spencer get back??"*

Below her text is a link to a news article.

From the headline alone I can tell that *another* girl has been found dead in the park. I'm fully awake now as I tap on the link, my eyes flicking hastily over the story.

My gaze settles on the image of the girl, and everything seems to go still.

The young woman in the article photo bears a striking similarity to the girl I saw Spencer with last night at the bar.

CHAPTER 20
SHANNON
SEVEN YEARS AGO

I don't know how much longer I can fake it.

This game of pretending that everything is okay. Spencer isn't home from work yet, but as the minutes drag on, I know it won't be long until he is.

I can practically feel the weight of his impending arrival beginning to collect across my shoulders. When I imagine having to smile at him, I shiver. He disgusts me.

More than that, he scares me.

Ever since the outburst, things have been different. Spencer seems perched on the edge, as if he could devolve into hysteria at any moment. Or maybe that's just my frantic imagination telling me that-at this point, I don't know *what* he might do.

It's been a long while since I've had a full night of sleep, and I can feel it.

I pick at my nailbeds as the seconds tick by. When he comes in, it'll be hours upon hours of time I'll have to spend with my husband who cheated on me. And I can't let on that anything is wrong, or there is no telling what he'll do.

A noise from the hallway brings my head up. Slow, plodding footsteps ambling their way toward the front door. Suddenly I realize I can't face Spencer, not right now.

I fly across the living room and slip into the bathroom as the sound of keys jingling in the hallway reaches my ears.

Hurriedly I tear off my clothes and turn on the shower, the water icy as it blasts out over me before warming.

I appreciate the shock actually—it grounds me, reminds me of how well I'll need to play my role until I can escape.

It won't be much longer now.

I've taken out enough money from our joint bank account that I'll be able to get out of New York and land somewhere else to start anew.

All that stands between me and leaving now is picking a day—and that's the hardest part.

I have a life here in the city. It's my home.

The front door swings open as Spencer's voice rings through the walls.

"I'm home!"

I shut my eyes and take a deep breath, the now-warm water washing over my face. Its steady pressure calms me a bit.

"Shannon, where are you?" Spencer shouts, "I've got a surprise for you."

Any sense of calm I'd been able to regain goes right out the window at that. My heart begins to thump in my chest. I can't take any more surprises from him.

"Shannon?"

Spencer is right outside the bathroom, sounding as if he's pressed himself up against the wood of the door.

"I'm in the shower, be out in a minute," I shout.

"Good. Come see my surprise," Spencer replies.

His voice is odd. Flat, almost.

My throat tightens as I'm forced to shut off the water. I have to face him now, there's no getting around it. It's impossible to know what waits for me on the other side of that door.

My mind fills with visions of my husband standing there, a loaded gun in his hand.

A sharp knife. Blood covering himself and the floor and the walls. Blinking hard, I work to get my breathing under control.

There's a robe hanging on the back of the door. Normally the warm fuzziness of it puts me in an instant state of relaxation, but not today. Not now.

I cinch the fabric belt of the robe with a shuddering breath. Is Spencer still waiting on the other side of the door?

Leaning forward, I try to be as quiet as possible as I press my ear to wood, damp with steamy condensation.

Steady breathing on the other side.

He's just standing there, waiting for me.

The lump in my throat grows larger and my heart contracts in a painful squeeze. *Who does that?*

Crazy thoughts fill my mind now. Would he really kill me? Did he find out about the money I withdrew?

The worst part is, there is nothing in here I could use to defend myself.

A quick scan of the misty bathroom reveals nothing more lethal than toilet paper and toothbrushes.

"You okay in there?" Spencer asks, his voice slicing through my thoughts.

He's waiting. Swallowing hard, I curl one hand into a fist and then reach forward to unlock the door. I'm almost moving in slow motion, not wanting to do it, but knowing I have to.

The door swings inward, revealing my husband standing there in his suit.

He looks up at me, giving me a large grin.

I can't tell if he's angry, or sad, or legitimately happy to see me, and that's utterly terrifying.

"Finally. Was beginning to think you slipped and fell in there. Then you wouldn't be able to see my surprise," he says.

I force a smile onto my face, though my entire body feels like doing nothing but screaming.

"What surprise?" I ask.

My voice quivers noticeably. Spencer, however, doesn't seem to notice as he steps forward and grabs hold of my forearm.

I'm practically yanked out of the bathroom, his fingers gripping my arm like a vice as he talks excitedly.

"The idea just hit me at work today—just landed right in my head like some sort of eureka moment, you know—and I knew instantly it was what had to happen. You wouldn't believe how energized I was, how ready to get out of work. Ended up leaving early, wait until you hear it—"

Suddenly I'm spun around and forced to face Spencer as he holds onto me.

My entire body trembles as my husband finds my eyes.

His are wide and moving quickly across my face.

"Are you ready for the surprise?"

"Oka—"

"I bought us tickets for a cruise," Spencer gushes, grinning wildly.

A cruise? That's what this is about?

My face must not be showing the level of excitement Spencer expects, and I can see his eyes darken momentarily in the low light of the living room.

"A second honeymoon—where we can renew our vows. A chance for us to reignite our love, pledge our loyalty to each other from here on out," he says.

"Unless… unless you don't love me anymore," he adds in a quiet voice.

As the words slip from between his lips, the grip on my forearm tightens. Hurriedly I shake my head.

"That-that sounds great, but I—"

Spencer nods quickly as he licks his lips. "Good. I knew you'd be onboard. I was so excited, I bought you something else, too. A gift."

He turns me again and points across the room toward the bedroom.

Standing in the doorway is a bright blue suitcase.

It's quite large, and definitely expensive.

Spencer finally releases me, taking a step forward with his arms out.

"So? What do you think? I had to go with that one–it matches my eyes. You've always said you love my eyes."

I swallow. "It's... very nice. But Spencer, what about work? What about—"

He waves me off. "I told them if they didn't give me the next seven days off, I was going to quit. We're free to set sail."

My eyes nearly pop out of my head. The next seven days? Then that means...

Spencer nods, seemingly following my train of thought, his smile growing wider by the second.

"That's right. We leave tomorrow night, soon as I get out of work. You and me, sailing off into the sunset."

A heavy feeling settles in the pit of my stomach as I glance toward the blue suitcase, a gift I might have loved at one point in our marriage.

Now I can't shake the feeling that if I go on that cruise with Spencer, I'll never be seen again.

My time has officially run out.

CHAPTER 21
ABBY

I swallow hard, blinking twice to clear the sleep from my eyes.

But it's unmistakable.

The article photograph shows a girl named Lexi Hardman wearing what seems to be an identical black puffer coat with a white furry hood as she poses with a friend.

Just like the girl Spencer was with last night.

Lexi's dark brown hair looks the same length, too. I swallow hard as I swipe over to my pictures and analyze the shot I took last night again.

That's the coat. The shot is a little blurry, but there's no mistaking it. My heartbeat pounds in my ears.

I read over the article with bloodshot eyes.

Lexi Hardman, aged twenty-four, was discovered in the early morning hours in Central Park. She worked as a paralegal.

Spencer came back late last night. My heart pounds. *The immediate shower.*

I'd assumed it had something to do with bodily fluids, but I didn't even consider blood.

I scroll back up to the picture of Lexi, unable to tear my

eyes away. She's laughing hard with a friend, both of them raising glasses in celebration of something.

My heart aches. When this photo was taken, Lexi thought she had her whole life ahead of her. Now she's a news story.

Back to the article. Like Elizabeth Waters, a chunk of Lexi's hair is missing. *Police now suspect it was the same killer in both instances, possibly a serial killer who takes a portion of the hair as some sort of trophy. Viral videos have dubbed the killer the Central Park Slayer.*

The words bounce around my skull as I stare at them. A lump forms in my throat. Spencer loves my hair, he used to tell me almost every day.

Behind me, the abrupt cut off of the shower snaps my head around toward the bathroom.

My heart is literally vibrating. Suddenly the flimsy door between us doesn't seem like enough.

If this *was* the same girl I saw last night—and I'm almost positive that it is—then it's the second time he's had direct contact with a murder victim.

I swallow hard and shakily put my phone down.

Spencer is stepping out of the shower. I dive back down to the covers, slamming my eyes shut and trying to keep my breathing as even as possible as I face away from the bathroom.

My ears strain for any noise from behind the door, but it's deathly quiet. Is he about to come out?

No, that's the buzz from his electric razor.

Clutching my phone to my chest, my mind races as I try to decide what to do next. The woman my husband was with last night was found dead in Central Park. I think.

It can't be just coincidence, can it?

I'm so exhausted, I can hardly think straight. My nerves are stretched thin. Should I go to the police? Again?

A cold chill washes over me at the realization that there's a virtual stranger standing feet away in my bathroom.

Not only is my husband a cheater, he very well might be a killer. Any desire I had to confront him about his adultery this morning has been sucked out of me like air on a spaceship.

The electric razor shuts off, plunging the apartment into silence once again.

What am I going to do?

I can hardly keep the phone in my hands, they're shaking so much. In the last few seconds I have before Spencer exits the bathroom, I open up my messages to fire off one to Katherine.

Looks like same—

The squeak of the door whips my head around. It's early, so the sunlight coming in through the windows is weak. Spencer has turned off the bathroom light, leaving only the night light on behind him.

It casts his naked, damp body in a strange glow. He's standing there, shoulders rising and falling as he watches me. I swallow around the lump in my throat. The phone remains clutched between my fingers, the text unsent.

"Morning, sweetheart. How are you feeling? I didn't wake you up, did I?"

It takes my brain a few moments to comprehend his words. He's talking to me. I should respond.

Finally I manage a shake of my head, though my throat is so tight I can hardly speak.

If I say the wrong thing, will he kill me too?

"No, I was already up," I say.

Spencer nods as he heads over to his closet.

"I've got that work thing in Chicago I was telling you about, that's why I'm up an hour earlier today. Sorry about the noise—couldn't find my travel toiletry bag," he says with a low chuckle.

Vaguely I'm able to dredge up a memory of him discussing the trip. A meeting with another office about something. Whatever it is, it really doesn't matter.

Not compared to what I know now.

"You okay?"

I glance over to find Spencer watching me again as he stands in front of his closet, a collared shirt suspended between his hands. Beads of water roll down his shoulders, dripping off the ends of his hair.

My chest tightens as I rack my brain for something to say.

Anything. Speak. Just open your mouth and talk.

"Still feeling a little out of it I think," I say, clearing my throat.

Spencer's eyebrows draw together in a look I would've previously taken to be sympathetic, but now I don't know.

Now he's walking toward me, and I can hardly breathe. It's all I can do to pray he doesn't notice me stiffening at his approach or hear my sudden intake of breath as his hand comes up to touch my forehead.

I need to breathe. If I don't, Spencer might think something is wrong beyond being under the weather. He might even kill me if he suspects I know what he's been up to..

Breathe Abby.

"Hmm. You don't feel too warm to me," he says.

Slowly my eyes come up to meet his. It feels like an eternity, the time spent with our eyes locked on each other. Does he know?

"Maybe you're getting over it then," he adds finally, snapping the tension and allowing me to exhale.

He straightens again and slides his arms into his shirt, talking to me as he buttons it.

"Take it easy for me today, okay? I'll check in once I get into Chicago."

I nod slowly, my skin still prickling from the sensation of his touch. Days ago, I couldn't get enough of it. Now, I want nothing more than to never be touched by him again, to be out of his presence as soon as possible.

Did he kill with those hands? Use them to slit the throat of some young girl in the dead of night?

I'm trembling, but Spencer is too busy inserting his cufflinks to notice.

"I'll be back early Sunday, okay?"

Swallowing, I nod again as he turns around to face me. Spencer regards me again, sending another panicky pulse through my body that has me sweating beneath my thin sleep shirt.

"Okay," I whisper because I know he's expecting me to say something in response.

"Okay. Bye. I love you," he says slowly.

He stands there another second, eyes holding mine. I know what he wants to hear me say, so I swallow down the painful lump in my throat.

"Love you too."

He knows something is up, I can just tell.

Spencer watches me another moment before stepping out of the bedroom and shutting the door behind him.

I remain upright in bed, listening to the sounds of him making eggs and coffee, unable to tear my eyes from the closed door. It's all that separates me from a potential murderer.

Who happens to be my husband.

Is it possible? I don't have the bandwidth to even consider the possibilities, not while Spencer is still in the apartment with me.

I hear the television click on, and an anchorman's voice fills the apartment.

"*—another woman found in Central Park this morning, in what appears to be the second victim of—*"

The TV switches off, plunging the apartment back into horrifying silence. I shut my eyes, feeling like Spencer is out there listening. Waiting to hear me breathing.

After another couple minutes, I hear the front door open and shut. The apartment goes still around me.

Even my own breathing stops for a moment. What if it's all a trick, and he's waiting just outside the bedroom door for me to come out?

He'll reveal he knows I emailed myself his conversations, tell me he knows I followed him. *That I'm next.*

But none of that happens. As the seconds tick on, I muster the courage to slip from the bed and make my way to the door. Pressing my cheek against the wood, I shut my eyes and listen again. There's nothing.

Gingerly I turn the doorknob.

The door comes open to reveal an empty apartment. Spencer's dirty dishes are out on the countertop for me to clean up.

He's gone for the next two days. Turning, I find that the TV actually hasn't been switched off entirely—just the volume has been muted.

On the screen is more footage of Central Park, yellow caution tape flapping in the spring breeze, before the picture switches back to the news studio.

Spencer saw the news coverage of the murder and decided to mute it.

What does that mean?

My head pounds as I stare numbly at the screen. Another tragic killing of another young girl. The girl my husband was out with last night.

I think I have to contact the police again.

What if it's all still just some crazy coincidence? Is that even possible?

I switch the volume back on, just in time to catch a sentence that sends a chill down my spine.

"*—missing, perhaps taken as a trophy.*"

The hair. In both cases, the victims had a chunk of their hair chopped off.

A chill settles over my skin. If Spencer is indeed the killer, then there's a good chance that hair might be in this apartment.

I take a shaking breath while rubbing my temples. I'm not crazy, am I?

Somehow I feel a little crazy for even thinking about it. A week ago, I would've called myself crazy for even considering my husband might be a killer. Now here we are.

My hand shakes a little as I pick up my phone to call the police.

I need to let them know my husband might be the Central Park Slayer.

CHAPTER 22
SPENCER

I don't like the way she looked at me.

Just now, in our bedroom, I sort of got the feeling that Abby knows more than she's letting on.

She couldn't know about me, could she? About what I've done?

I pause in the hallway, the seconds ticking away loudly in my mind. Abby has just turned the television volume back on, listening to the story about that thing in the park.

My pulse quickens. She waited until I was gone before leaving bed, acting as if she were so sick she could hardly move. Then the second I leave, she pops right up?

Something isn't right.

As gently as I can, I turn and go to stand right outside our apartment door. The muffled noise of the television is even louder now, but still I hear her voice.

Sounds like she's talking to someone in there. On the phone, maybe?

I readjust my grip on my briefcase so I can lean forward and press my ear to the door. I don't know what I'm expecting to hear, but I definitely don't hear Abby talking anymore.

My breathing gets slow, steady. My calmness impresses me, given the circumstances.

It only takes me another second to realize not all of the breaths I hear are mine.

Abby is on the other side of the door listening, too.

She must've heard me walking back to the apartment. I straighten up instantly, pulse quickening as my mind races to determine what to do. If she starts to question me, I'm dead.

There's no way I'll be able to keep up the act any longer.

A brilliant idea hits me—the same one that worked with Shannon.

My fingers wrap around the door handle and yank the door open in a flash, revealing Abby frozen in a half-lean, her face jerking up to mine with wide eyes.

She really was listening.

She must know something.

No, she doesn't. You're so smart. Smarter than her, smarter than Shannon. Think.

"What are you doing?" I ask in a loud voice.

If I ask first, the onus is on her to answer. Abby is backing away, her cheeks coloring.

Pulling away from me. Just like Shannon.

Hot whips of panic begin to yank at the corners of my mind, tugging at it like balls of yarn, threatening to unwind the whole thing.

She's got her phone in her hand, and she's definitely on the line with someone.

"Who are you calling?" I ask, heart pounding.

If it's who I think it is, there's going to be trouble.

"I—" Abby stutters.

She's flustered, which gives me a shot of strength, allows me to tamper down the terror building inside me.

"Katherine," she stammers, "I was calling her to see if she could pick up something for me at the pharmacy for my cold."

My pulse slows a little. Swallowing, I throw out a question.

"Is something wrong? Why were you standing at the door?"

The words sit in the air. Heavy. I search her eyes, trying to dig the truth out of her.

These women in my life always seem to betray me, always seem to have secrets. I learned I couldn't trust Shannon.

Can I trust Abby?

"I just… I thought I heard footsteps, but you didn't come in. I… was wondering if you forgot something," she says.

There's a visible sheen of sweat across her forehead.

Is she really sick, or is that suspicion manifest?

I swallow again. It's a logical explanation. Now I have to come up with one to explain why I came back.

My eyes flick around the kitchen for only a moment—that's all the time I need, given how smart I am—and then the solution comes. My shoulders relax as I tip my chin toward one of the cabinets.

"I forgot Advil. You know how airports always give me a headache. The reason I didn't open the door right away is that I worried you were still sleeping. Didn't want to wake you."

It's a perfect lie, and Abby knows it too. She nods rapidly.

"Right. That was… considerate."

I step forward again, my expensive leather dress shoes letting out a small squeak. I notice Abby has hung up her phone call.

Opening my arms, I beckon for her to come to me. After a moment's hesitation, she does.

It sends a wave of relief through me. I still have control. Not like with Shannon. I can fix this.

This time, things will be different.

Abby leans into my chest as my arms wrap around her back. I shift my hand up to her head and begin gently stroking her hair as I gaze out the windows on the other side of the apartment.

"Everything is going to be fine," I say.

I know she loves to feel the reverberation of my voice in my chest. But really, the words are more for me than for her. It's a reassurance to myself that things won't end up the way they did with Shannon.

Abby doesn't respond. She doesn't even murmur a word. That isn't normal.

A slow chill snakes its way up my spine as I continue to stroke her hair like nothing has changed.

But I know it has. She doesn't believe me. Just like Shannon. My jaw tightens as I forcibly prevent myself from collapsing into raw panic. It takes every fiber of my being to continue to breathe slowly, evenly.

Stroking my wife's hair.

Stroking my wife's hair and knowing that I've got to do something.

And as the two of us stand there in our kitchen, I realize I know just what to do.

CHAPTER 23
ABBY

Spencer left nearly thirty minutes ago, but I still have yet to recover.

He was listening. Listening while I called the police. It's truly a miracle I didn't get past the front desk and say something that would've let him know I knew.

I hold up my hand, watching as it trembles in front of me.

My own husband makes me shake in fear. What a nightmare reality has become.

And the hug. I shudder as I see him in my mind, standing there, arms wide and waiting. When he touched my hair, I nearly screamed.

I've got the police on the phone again. This time, I'm absolutely certain Spencer is gone.

I've been on hold for almost fifteen minutes while they connect me with detectives working the case.

Let's hope it isn't Sullivan and Marsh.

"This is Detective Sullivan, with whom am I speaking?" comes the voice through the phone's speaker, dashing my hopes.

Doesn't matter what I think of the man—I've got to tell them about what I found out.

"Yes, hi... this is Abby Stevens, I'm not sure if you'll remember me. I—"

"Hello Mrs. Stevens, I remember you," Sullivan says, interrupting me, "I've been told you have a possible new lead on the killing in the park?"

"Yes," I breathe, "my husband—he was out last night with another girl. I'm almost positive it was Lexi Hardman, the girl found today in the park."

A second of silence passes.

"Why would you think that?"

"I saw them together—last night. And he didn't come home until very late."

"You're absolutely sure it was her you saw with him?"

I bite my lip.

"Well, not exactly... I mean, I never saw her face. But the coats were identical, and her hair seemed the same, too. And like I said, Spencer came back super late."

Saying it out loud, it doesn't sound nearly as cut and dried as it did inside my head.

I can practically see the look pass between Sullivan and Marsh before the man responds.

"I see, Mrs. Stevens. We appreciate the information."

"That's it?" I ask, my heart pounding. "Don't you want to look into him? He took a shower last night, too."

"He took a shower?" Sullivan asks.

He clears his throat. "Listen, Mrs. Stevens, I'm sorry about your husband, I really am. It's a terrible thing what he's doing to you, just ain't right. But without revealing too much...our investigation is leading us in another direction."

And that's that—I'm off the phone, sitting there staring at the wall with the detective's words bouncing around my mind.

It's clear they aren't taking me or Katherine seriously.

I switch the TV back on as I give my temples a rub to try and ease the pounding in my brain. All the talk is still on the two slayings, though now it seems to be centered on the idea of the Central Park Slayer, and the hair taken from the victims.

Resolution settles across my brow. That's it.

I'll do a search of the apartment. Every square inch of it, if I have to. I need to know the truth, once and for all.

I need to know if my husband is a killer.

It's pitch black outside the apartment by the time I finally raise my head and look up from my task.

My stomach rumbles as I wipe the sweat from my brow, heart beating a little faster from the exertion of moving aside the drawers. Licking my lips, I hungrily slurp down a glass of mineral water from the refrigerator.

The apartment is in a state of total disarray. Sheets, cushions and pillows lay scattered across the floor. The rugs have been rolled up and now lean against the walls. Every piece of furniture has been moved from its initial position.

If Spencer were to come back now, there would be no excuse for this place.

But he isn't here.

And apparently, he isn't a killer either.

Either that, or he's a smart one with better hiding places than his place of residence. Even after hours of searching, I haven't found anything suspicious.

As I open the vanity cabinet and catch sight of the tampon box, my stomach tightens. The pictures aren't there anymore, but the tears in the cardboard remain. It began with messages, and now I search for proof of murder. From utterly adoring my husband to absolutely fearing him in a matter of days.

Is that why he looked at me for so long this morning, as if he was able to see straight through my eyes to my thoughts? Could he see the transition?

A twinge of relief wants to make a home inside me at not finding anything, but some part of me still won't let it go. Just because the girls' hair isn't here doesn't rule out Spencer entirely. He really could have it stashed someplace else.

How many spouses are even aware of all the places their loved ones go when they leave home for the day?

How jaded I've become.

Before, I defended Spencer to Katherine, even in the face of the obvious.

Now, it seems as though I've swung all the way to the opposite side.

I finish the glass of water before setting it back down on the countertop. With another glance around the living room, I decide there simply isn't a place left to check.

If Spencer does have the clipped hair sections, they are hidden somewhere I can't find them.

I need to eat something, otherwise I might faint. It's been a long day of stressful, strenuous activity, and I'm exhausted both physically and mentally.

The worst part is, I don't even know what to believe anymore. I almost wanted to find something, just to end this torture of not-knowing.

Katherine responds quickly to my invitation to come over for food. I take another quick look around the apartment and can't help but cringe. It looks like a tornado came through and blew the place apart.

It's a perfect representation of my life these days. Fitting, really.

I probably look even worse, but it doesn't really matter since we're going to order in. I know Katherine won't judge.

Thirty minutes later, I'm standing at the corner of my block, shivering in the darkness. My coat is buttoned up and pulled tight around me, but it isn't nearly enough to combat the brutal wind that cuts through me like a knife.

Across the street is the subway stop Katherine uses when she comes over to visit. I grit my teeth as I check my phone screen for the time. She's late, and I'm freezing.

Where is she? At this point, I'm starving.

I open up my phone again, intending to threaten that I'll order without her if she doesn't arrive soon.

"Stupid subway car stopped in the middle of the stupid tunnel for some reason." Katherine's voice draws my head up. She's walking toward me.

"Late," I scold, tucking my phone away.

"Blame the MTA," Katherine says before pulling me into a hug.

I melt into her, shutting my eyes tight as we embrace. Without my permission, tears begin to fill my eyes, and then I'm crying.

Katherine pulls back to look at me, her eyes scanning my face.

"What's wrong?"

"Everything," I manage between sniffles.

The people on the sidewalk around us spare little more than disinterested glances at my waterworks before continuing onward. That's the good and the bad thing about NYC. Life goes on, with or without you.

As we walk back toward my building, I fill Katherine in on the phone call with the police, and my subsequent demolition of the apartment, all of it to no avail.

Her face is ghostly white by the time I wrap up the summary of my day so far. People continue to stream past us, oblivious to the chaos and confusion my life has become.

"This is…" Katherine starts before trailing off.

I bite my lip and nod. There aren't really words to describe the situation.

"Where is Spencer now?" she asks.

"He's on this work trip, won't be back for a couple days."

Katherine shakes her head. "That Detective Sullivan—he's a real piece of work, isn't he? Taking the investigation in another direction. Yeah, the *wrong* one."

"I wish I had seen her face," I say between chattering teeth, "Then I'd know for sure. If only I'd stayed a little longer. It just hurt so much to see them."

Katherine squeezes my arm. "No one is blaming you, believe me."

We reach the front doors of my building, and she tilts her head back and looks up at my apartment window.

"And nothing came from the search, huh?"

I shake my head. "Nothing. Now I've got to put the whole place back together again. It's a disaster area. I can't let Spencer come home and find it that way."

"I'll help you," Katherine says.

"Really?" I can't keep the obvious delight out of my voice. I could really use the help, and I was kind of hoping she'd offer, if I'm being honest.

"Of course. I don't mind."

We head inside the building, relieved at the sudden blast of heat in the lobby area. In the elevator we make a quick decision on what to eat and place an order for delivery.

When I open the door to the apartment, Katherine steps inside and lets out a whistle.

She lowers her purse to the countertop before taking a few steps into the living room.

"Now this is a strip search," she says in a tone that sounds almost like admiration.

"Too bad it was pointless," I mutter. "Reconsidering your offer to help?"

Katherine lowers herself to a squat and rubs a knot in the floorboards.

"Decent place, if it weren't for the complete idiot living here."

I nod. "Even though I didn't find anything, I don't think I can sleep here again. Not with the thoughts going through my head."

Just because I didn't find the hair doesn't mean that Spencer had nothing to do with the deaths of the two girls. I'm suspicious of everything now. How much has changed in so little time.

"You said he came back late last night, right?" she asks.

I nod. "Yeah. It was nearly dawn."

Katherine nods. "Did it sound like he was rummaging around in here or anything?"

It's hard to recall every detail of last night, which feels so far away now.

I was so emotionally shattered at the sight of Spencer with the girl that I could hardly think straight, let alone track his movements when he got back.

And I'm so tired now after not sleeping—again. Shutting my eyes, I try to remember what I heard when Spencer came home.

Did he spend long in the living room?

I feel like I'm trying to squeeze the memories out of my exhausted brain by force.

No, I decide.

"I don't think so," I say to Katherine. "I'm pretty sure he came in and got right in the shower."

She chews her lip but says nothing.

"Is there a chance I've got this all wrong? That it's just some horrible coincidence?" I ask, the panicky words bursting out of me in a rush.

I somehow feel wracked with guilt and utterly terrified at the same time.

Guilty for even thinking Spencer could be capable of something like this—and absolute terror that it might be true.

Katherine eyes me for a moment as she appears to be choosing her words carefully.

No doubt she's thinking back to our conversation at the bar.

"You already know what I think," she says.

Her words settle like a load of bricks in my stomach. I want to scream that it can't be true, that I know Spencer.

And yet, the past week's discoveries have proven I really don't.

Is it possible I chose my husband so poorly? That would make me a hopeless fool, wouldn't it?

Tears spring up in the corners of my eyes as I stand there in the kitchen, grappling with the reality that everything I believed about my life is a lie.

Katherine steps forward and gives my shoulder a squeeze.

"I'm sorry," she says in a quiet voice. "Listen, why don't you stay with me tonight? I don't like the idea of you being here all alone tonight either."

Sniffling, I give her a nod. It would be nice to not be by myself right now. She rubs my shoulder then sets down her glass.

"How about this—we have at least twenty minutes before the food gets here. Let's do a last search as we put things back together, and then you stay with me tonight," Katherine says.

I nod at her gratefully.

She goes to use the bathroom while I dig through my closet for my weekend bag. I almost don't want to let her out of my sight, as if being alone will mean I get lost in the mess of this apartment and my mess of a life.

Lost is the perfect word for how I feel about everything right now.

Darkness seems to creep inside the apartment despite all the lamps I've got on, working its way out of the corners to plunge everything into confusion.

We move the furniture back into place, and I dig in the couch cushions one more time, just in case I missed something.

As we reload the cabinets and drawers, Katherine takes

off the lids and peeks inside of any container that could possibly hold anything of interest.

It's all a repeat, but I don't mind. With Katherine here and helping me, I feel less insane. It's not all just in my head, like the police seem to believe.

If Katherine thinks there could be some truth to my thoughts, then there is.

After a conclusive search of the kitchen, living room, and bedroom, we determine definitively that there are no hidden caches of hair. Katherine leans back against the counter and sips a glass of mineral water.

"Well, it was worth a try. Your apartment is habitable now, at least. Want to start packing?"

Her eyes fall to my weekend bag laying on the corner of the bed.

"Sure," I say.

Then a thought hits me. My eyes lock onto all the zippered pockets on the black leather bag. I swallow, suddenly imagining hair stuffed into one of them–I hadn't thought to check my *own* things when I did my initial search.

Suddenly I'm moving into the bathroom, my pulse quickening.

"What?" Katherine asks from the kitchen.

When I get to the vanity cabinet, I pull open the first drawer. It's Spencer's and I've already looked it over.

But I didn't check my own drawer. There was no reason to, unless...

Pulling open the second drawer, my body stills.

My vacation toiletry bag. It is stuffed up against the back, the front facing toward me.

That's when I notice it. The long, dark strand of hair poking out from between the zippered teeth.

My pulse is so loud it makes it hard to think.

No. It can't be.

"Katherine," I shout.

Blinking hard, I point a shaking hand toward the errant piece of hair sticking out from between the zipper. Katherine glances over at me, eyes wide. My chest pounds.

Neither of us speak as she reaches in and cautiously unzips the bag.

Nestled inside are two braids of hair.

CHAPTER 24
ABBY

I can hardly manage to remain standing.

These are *the* braids of hair. What the police have been looking for.

One is blonde, like Elizabeth Waters. The second is dark brown, just like the hair of Lexi Hardman, who was found today.

The same girl Spencer was with last night. *The girl he killed.*

Proof of his evil deeds is sitting right there on top of my things. Ridiculing me. When he told me he grabbed his toiletry kit out of the vanity this morning, I thought nothing of it.

In actuality, he was stuffing his crimes into his wife's vacation toiletry bag. Hiding horror in plain sight.

Gripping the sink for support, I take a deep breath.

Only then do I realize Katherine is saying something beside me, her lips moving a mile a minute.

There's so much going on in my head, I can't for the life of me figure out what she's saying.

I manage to tune in midstream.

"—have to call someone right now, Abby. I mean, like, I thought… but I didn't actually—"

The police. We have to tell the police. My gaze goes back to my bag sitting so innocently on the cabinet shelf.

Something I've looked at a thousand times. Something I've brought with me all over the country. A piece of me that is now a vessel for atrocity.

"What are you doing?" Katherine asks me, snapping me back to reality.

She's got her hand wrapped around my wrist. I blink and then realize my hand was just a few inches from the bag.

"I've got to make sure…"

She shakes her head. "Abby, this is evidence of two *murders*. You shouldn't touch it. I shouldn't have touched it with my bare hands to open it," she says.

She's right, as horrible as it is. The truth comes crashing down in one breath as the reality of a police investigation here in my apartment finally sets in.

I can't keep pretending. The murders that happened on the news—the man who committed them lives right here.

My husband.

The next few hours are a blur. Katherine dialed the police at some point, and then things started moving very fast.

Now I'm sitting on the couch as men and women in blue jackets swarm my apartment like bugs.

They're searching over everything in a similar manner to the way Katherine and I did earlier, only they know what they're doing. If there's any more evidence to be found here, *they* won't miss it.

My gaze drifts over to the kitchen, where a woman with a tight bun is rummaging through the trash with blue gloves on. She pulls out a cup and says something to the man beside her before bagging it.

Someone squeezes my hand. I glance over to see Katherine, who gives me another supportive squeeze. I feel completely numb. Shell-shocked.

A bomb has been dropped on my life and completely decimated it. Not only was Spencer cheating on me, he was killing women, too.

It's such an awful reality to face that I truly can't even comprehend it.

The only thing I know for sure is this—Spencer is not the man I thought I married.

"—went into the bathroom to search, but then realized she hadn't looked through her own things," Katherine says beside me, repeating what she told another detective earlier about how I found out the truth.

"And so she opened the drawer," Detective Sullivan continues as he scribbles into his notebook.

I notice he hasn't made eye contact with me since arriving with his team.

"She opened the drawer, and then called me in. Right from her tone, I knew something was wrong. There was her bag, lying there. Then I unzipped the bag—"

"You unzipped the bag?"

Katherine nods. "Yeah. I unzipped the bag. Sorry, Detective Sullivan, but *someone* had to solve this thing."

Detective Sullivan diverts his eyes as he makes another mark in his notebook. After clearing his throat, he looks up at me.

"And Mrs. Stevens… you said uh, you said your husband is out of town, correct?"

He's asked me a question. I should respond. I want to answer, but it seems like my voice is missing. Katherine squeezes my hand again, spurring me onward.

"Yes. He'll be back in two days," I manage in a tiny voice.

Sullivan writes that down too.

"Thank you. That's all I need for now," the man says before standing up off the couch and straightening his tie.

I expect him to walk away, but he doesn't. Instead, he turns back around to us and licks his lips.

"Listen, I…" he starts but stops without finishing.

Then he heads for the kitchen. The heels of his dress shoes clop across the floor as he goes, a hand running through his thinning hair.

The sound of his footfalls echoes distantly in my ears as Katherine shakes her head.

"How that moron has a job is beyond me. We basically handed everything to him, and he still wouldn't believe us."

There are so many emotions swirling inside me that I can't look at anyone, or I'll collapse. I need to retreat inward, bottle all this up before it spills out and I go down the drain with it.

Never mind the police. How could *I* have missed something like this?

Spencer was able to hide an entire double life from me, cheating and killing behind my back while I loved him and cooked for him.

I loved him like nothing else—always had, from the moment I laid eyes on him.

"Maybe this'll force these halfwits to look into Shannon, too," Katherine says beside me.

I don't respond, for fear if I open my mouth, I might burst into tears in front of all these people. It's all too much.

Distantly I hear Katherine calling for someone's attention, and then her words drift down to me as she goes over the details of Shannon's disappearance again.

"Everyone says she ran away, but come on, take a look around," she says.

"Understood, Ms. May. thank you," a woman replies.

My head drops and I bury my face in my hands. I feel weak, drained. I have no strength left.

In my mind, I see Spencer's smile as he gently braids my hair on the couch. The two of us sharing leftover takeout that was questionably old. The clean, dark smell of his cologne when he hugs me in one of his lovely suits.

How can this be the same man who killed those girls and left them in the park?

I never really knew Spencer. I never really knew my husband.

Looks like that old phrase really is true, as much as I hate to admit it. No one really knows anyone after all.

We shared everything with each other—or so I thought.

Was there ever anything real about our love?

Katherine's face comes into my view and pulls me out of my thoughts.

"I'm going to try and talk to Sullivan again about Shannon, okay?" she says, leaning forward so she can see my eyes. "Are you good here on the couch?"

I nod. "Yeah, I think so."

She pulls me into another hug. "I'll be just a second, and then we'll go to my place for the night while the police figure this out."

She steps into the bedroom in pursuit of Detective Sullivan. With her gone, I feel exposed again. I'm not alone, but there are so many unknown faces in my apartment that I might as well be.

All of them move about with purpose, bagging things and snapping photos as I watch.

My life will never be the same again.

A strange noise jars me from my thoughts and pulls my attention toward the kitchen.

That's the front door, a key jiggling inside the lock.

My brow furrows as my mind works to try and understand what's going on. Spencer isn't due back for another couple days.

There are two police officers in the living room with me, but they're over by the windows engaged in quiet conversation.

The detectives are in the bathroom, the bedroom door separating us halfway shut.

There's nothing I can do but watch as the door to our apartment swings open, and Spencer steps inside.

CHAPTER 25
ABBY

The next few moments are surreal.

Spencer comes into the apartment with a half-smile on his face, mouth opening as if he's about to speak when he catches sight of the state of the place.

Strangely enough, he's rolling a large red suitcase behind him.

The two officers behind me spot him, and then everyone starts shouting.

I'm frozen on the couch, my mouth hanging open as the chaos unfolds. The detectives sprint out of the bedroom, guns drawn on Spencer as his head whips wildly back and forth.

"What's going on?" he shouts as the police scream at him to drop his duffel bag.

His arms shoot up into the air, and the cops draw closer, their boots clattering on the hardwood floor. The suitcase topples over, forgotten in the anarchy.

"Get down, right now," one of the officers shouts in a harsh tone.

Spencer remains standing as he looks between all of them, apparently too confused to comply.

"What is this?" he asks.

He's still clutching his duffel bag in one hand, his suit jacket in the other. Both are raised over his head.

"Get on the ground," the man shouts again.

Then Spencer's gaze moves past the police officers and finds me.

My body goes rigid as his intense blue eyes bore into me.

"Abby, what's going on?" he asks in a quiet voice as if it's just the two of us.

There's a strange tremble to it I've never heard from him before.

My chest tightens. No words come out in response. Spencer's attention remains locked on me as the police rush forward and force him down to the kitchen tile.

The duffel bag is wrenched from his grasp.

Spencer blinks hard, finally breaking the connection with my eyes to twist his head around and ask again what's happening.

The officers don't answer, ignoring him as they wrestle his arms behind him and into handcuffs.

"The braids, Spencer," I say suddenly, surprising even myself.

Somehow, I've found my voice. Spencer snaps back over to me, his brow furrowing.

"What braids?"

The cop with his knee digging into Spencer's back scoffs.

"Abby, what braids?" Spencer asks, his voice raising an octave.

I guess I spoke because I wanted to see his face. Wanted to hear him admit to the truth of his horrifying behavior. But now that I'm looking at him, I just want to crawl into a hole and ignore the world forever. This is a nightmare.

Spencer finally seems to make the connection as he's hauled up to his feet. When he does, things change.

It's like a transformation occurs, and the Spencer I've known... alters.

His eyes widen, and he starts to buck against the officers holding him.

"No," he screams in a shrill voice I've never heard before.

"Enough," one of them shouts, his jaw tightening as my husband begins to practically seize in their grasp.

"No," Spencer screams, "This isn't happening."

His voice does not sound like the man I know, and somehow that scares me even more. It shocks the officers too, who momentarily lose their grip and allow Spencer to go crashing back down to the floor.

Without his arms to brace his fall, he lands hard, but the impact doesn't stop him. If anything, he's writhing even more now, and slamming his head down against the tile floor with thuds that make my stomach clench.

It takes the officers half a second to comprehend what is even happening.

Moments before, this man was smiling.

Now he's thrashing around on the floor like a wild animal, literally kicking and screaming as he devolves.

One of them dives on top of him to try and get Spencer to stop slamming his head into the floor.

It's a mess of limbs and shouted commands as more cops stream in from the other rooms to help subdue Spencer's mania.

It takes four of them, but finally they're able to haul him back up to his feet. When our eyes meet again, I don't recognize him.

Blood rushes down his face from a cut across his forehead. The red streaks run down over his eyes, cheeks and mouth, creating a horrifying image that burns itself into my mind.

"Abby—Abby, how could you," he shouts over to me.

He sounds so hurt, so betrayed. But the way he's looking and acting now, I can't trust a word of it.

Spit flies from his mouth, tinged red with the blood that's run over his lips.

"My life was supposed to be special," he yells. "We were supposed to be special."

I flinch at the words, each of them striking me to the core.

I did think he was special once.

I thought we had something special. Now I can't look at him. I don't know if I ever can again.

They're carting him out the door now, but not without effort. Spencer bucks hard against the cops, throwing his head wildly back and forth then twisting back to look at me over his shoulder.

"No," he screams, thrashing. "I got you a gift. This isn't how it's supposed to go. Abby!"

"Stop resisting," one of the officers shouts, and then there's a grunt as something strikes Spencer.

He sags forward and is finally pulled through the door. I let out a shaky breath, thinking it's finally over, but then I hear him screaming my name again from the hall as they drag him toward the elevator.

Shutting my eyes, I try to block out his cries. He's out there shouting my name, over and over again as if I'm going to charge the police and rescue him, after all he's done.

Who is this man I thought I knew? He's not even sane.

Sullivan steps over to me, sweat beads dotting his temples as he pants slightly.

"Sorry, Mrs. Stevens. You shouldn't have had to—"

"You're right she shouldn't have," Katherine hisses as she steps back over to me and wraps her arms around me protectively. "If you'd done your jobs, that second girl wouldn't be dead, either."

I don't say anything. I can't. All I can do is picture Spencer in the elevator, screaming my name and wrestling with the police officers. My handsome husband, still in his suit pants and dress shirt.

His duffel bag and suit jacket remain on the floor in the

kitchen like debris. The red suitcase, too. I can't tear my eyes away from it.

Sullivan's gaze bounces back and forth between Katherine and me, and he makes the wise decision to quietly step away.

She hands me a glass of water which I accept with trembling hands.

"Well. That was something," she says simply as she shakes her head.

She sounds unnerved. I feel the same way. That behavior was not something I'd ever seen from my husband before. It was like a different person took over his body.

I guess when faced with the truth, the mask fell away, and the true Spencer was revealed.

I sip the water, feeling it rush down my dry throat and hit my stomach. I don't manage more than a couple sips though before feeling as if I might vomit, so I set the glass down on the coffee table.

Katherine is talking with the officers again, probably telling them that I'll be spending the night at her place. One of them looks over at me during the conversation, his face impassive.

I stare back at him blankly until he looks away. I don't know my husband. I don't know myself.

We walk in silence to the subway stop.

It's a wonder I manage to put one foot in front of the other. My whole body feels numb. The journey back to Katherine's place is something of a blur.

When we finally step inside her place, I feel ready to collapse. She's got a studio, which means her place is only one room, but it's cozy. Cozy is what I need right now.

"You can stay here as long as you need to," Katherine says as she places two fluffy pillows on the couch.

I nod my thanks, unable to voice a reply around the lump in my throat.

Katherine's cat stares at me as I lie there, completely lost to the emotional storm taking place within me. Somehow, despite everything that's happened, my thoughts keep returning to Spencer and how he must be feeling, locked up wherever they took him.

Why do I even care? He's a dirty cheater and a bad man.

Something must be wrong with me.

"I've got to go in early tomorrow, so if you wake up and I'm not here, that's where I am, okay? Just text me if you need anything, and I'll reply as quickly as I can," Katherine says.

I'm staring blankly at the pillows, hardly even hearing her. In my mind, I'm rewinding my fifth date with Spencer, the first time I stayed over at his place.

We spent all night just looking at each other, staring into each other's eyes and talking the hours away as we rested against the pillows until our necks were sore.

"Abby," Katherine repeats, drawing me from my thoughts.

I stir and glance toward her. "Uh, yeah. Thanks."

She pulls me into another hug and then wishes me good night.

I'm a little relieved when she gets into her bed and goes quiet. As grateful as I am for her, I don't want to face the world anymore. I just need some time to cry quietly to myself.

That's exactly what I do, tossing and turning in the sheets of my makeshift bed as I succumb to grief.

I have absolutely no idea what is supposed to come next.

CHAPTER 26
ABBY

Waking up the next morning, I almost feel hungover like I did after all those drinks that night at the bar.

There's a crater in my chest, like a missile has been launched and blown up my entire life. My sleep was poor at best, filled with Spencer desperately crying my name as they dragged him out into the hallway.

Even in the face of obvious, overwhelming evidence, he was still pleading with me. He was still trying to convince me of his innocence.

I open my eyes and shake my head.

That's just the part of me that still loves him, wanting to believe whatever he says.

I guess those feelings don't just disappear overnight, but I refuse to be one of those wives of serial killers who keep their heads in the sand and defend their husbands till the end, despite all the blatant truth that proves otherwise.

The braids were found in *our* vanity cabinet, after he had direct contact with *both* girls. That's pretty conclusive.

I just need to try my best not to think about it.

Sitting up on Kathrine's couch, and looking around at the four walls, I realize holing away in her apartment and isolating myself from the world is a one-way ticket to obsessive thoughts. About everything.

Her place is nice, but I'll go stir crazy if I have to sit here for hours waiting for her to come home from work. No, I need to be outside. I need fresh air.

I need to go out and be among people, though I hardly want to show my face. At least out there I can hope to get distracted by the noise of the city, which is guaranteed to be there twenty-four-seven.

Maybe a walk through the busy city streets will at least fracture my attention and keep the events from yesterday from running through my head in a continuous loop.

After going to the bathroom and blowing my nose, I shuffle back into the living area. I don't dare turn on the news or even get near the TV. I know exactly what it'll say.

Businessman Spencer Stevens identified as Central Park Slayer, arrested in shocking murders of two women found in Central Park.

The last thing I need right now is to see my husband's handsome face splashed across the screen above those terrible words.

After Spencer revealed his first wife had disappeared and told me his side of the story, I honestly never had the urge to check the news about it.

Maybe that was naive, but Spencer swore he was telling me the truth, and I believed him.

I just figured there was no point in seeking out speculation and gossip from people who'd never met him and weren't even involved. Outsiders, who didn't have all the information.

I knew all I needed to know and trusted Spencer implicitly.

Looking back on it now, I think maybe I just didn't *want* to think about what had happened with his first wife.

Burying my head in the sand. Forgetting about it.

I blow my nose again as a wave of hunger hits me.

Katherine was nice enough to leave some clothes out for me, one of my own sweatshirts and a pair of sweatpants from the last time I stayed over during one of Spencer's work trips.

I slip into the comfy clothes and make my way back to the bathroom to splash some water on my face before leaving in search of breakfast and human companionship.

A look in the mirror reflects heavy bags underneath sad, sunken eyes that make me look years older. Dark purple smudges make me look like I've been carrying the weight of the world for decades instead of only days.

My hair needs help too, but there isn't much I can do besides brushing it. I stare at my reflection as I drag the brush through the knots in my hair.

At each painful tug, I notice the person staring back at me doesn't so much as wince at the pain.

Blessed numbness doing its thing, keeping me breathing.

I find a trench coat of Katherine's hanging on a rack and slip into it. I know she won't mind me borrowing it. Tying the belt in a knot around my waist, I take a deep breath and pull open the door to her apartment.

I don't know what I expect to see in the hallway—thousands of reporters, flashing cameras, police lights? But it's empty. My stomach rumbles now, loudly enough that it makes me bring a hand up to cover it.

With everything that happened last night, I didn't end up eating anything. Not as if I would've had much of an appetite. Now is a different story.

I already know where I'll go.

My comfort cafe, Mud Pot. A place I know I'll be cozy and safe. It's a much farther walk to the cafe from Katherine's place than mine, but I don't mind it.

It's a chance to focus on something other than my own pounding thoughts. Without my earbuds in, I'm privy to all the shrill honking and shouting and beeping that makes up the soundtrack of New York City.

The chorus of sounds and random bits of conversation help keep me afloat, reminding me I'm just one of millions walking the streets today. Life will go on regardless of how it feels right now.

It's drizzling rain outside, which makes me wish I'd at least checked the weather on my phone before leaving the apartment. Oh well.

I flip up the collar on the trench coat and hunch my shoulders inward, feeling cold drops of water splash down onto my scalp as I hug myself for warmth. Slick puddles on the street reflect an overcast sky back to me, mirroring my mood.

I already know exactly what to order when I get to the cafe, and where I'm going to sit to eat it. Hopefully Rachel's working today too. I could definitely use a warm smile.

I envision the sensation of delicious food in my stomach, and the comforting routine of sipping on a strong cup of caffeine.

That'll be the first step of many it'll take to get through the challenges of the next few days.

One at a time, Abby. One at a time.

After a lengthy walk, I catch sight of the cafe as it appears out of the mist up ahead.

It's not too busy right now, seeing as the morning rush has passed.

The lunch crowd won't be in for another few hours.

The doorbell dings overhead as a step inside and let out a shiver, shaking off a few droplets of water before casting a glance around the interior of the place.

Behind the counter, Rachel talks with another girl. It's Hannah, the same one from the other day.

Neither of them turns toward me as I come in, deep in conversation with each other.

I step up to the counter, and Rachel pulls her attention away from her friend to focus on me.

"Oh, hey Abby," she says.

She looks a little pale. I'm sure I don't look fantastic either, so no judgement here.

I muster up a smile as if everything is okay and raise a hand in greeting back to her.

"Morning."

Surprisingly, my voice comes out sounding more chipper than I thought possible. I guess I'm pretty good at faking it, if I have to.

There are just a few other patrons in the restaurant beside me, all of them quietly talking among themselves or looking at their phones as they eat.

Though they have no idea who I am, I can't help but imagine all of them turning to me and pointing, announcing that the wife of the murderer Spencer Stevens has arrived.

My eyes are drawn to the television hanging in the corner to my right. I only catch a second of it before looking away hurriedly. Of course it's about the arrest.

I swallow hard, ready to give the order I rehearsed a hundred times on the way over so I wouldn't forget. Rachel is talking again with Hannah beside her in a hushed voice. I see Hannah's eyes flicker up to the TV before she shakes her head gravely.

Suddenly Rachel turns to me again, as if she's forgotten I was there.

"So sorry—a little scrambled today," she says with a shake of her head, "The usual?"

That makes two of us. Scrambled doesn't even begin to cover my state.

With another small smile and a nod, I head away from the counter and slide into a booth by the window.

I need caffeine right now like I need air to breathe.

So many nights of restless sleep have left me feeling brittle and unable to think straight, which is not how I need to be feeling at a time like this.

At least I feel a little better now that I'm in my usual spot, tucked away where I usually get my best work done.

Oh, God. *Work*.

There's something I haven't thought about in days. With everything that's been going on, my job has been the last thing on my mind. They must think I've fallen off the face of the earth or quiet-quit or something.

I pull up my email and feel my stomach tighten as my gaze falls on a message from my boss asking if I'm okay.

That's when I realize everyone at my job already knows why I've gone AWOL.

No doubt they've seen the news like the rest of the city.

I close my email. I can't handle any sort of questions or half-hearted pity that thinly disguises curious prying from my coworkers.

Slumping into the seat cushion, I let my fingers trace the familiar grooves in the table and I stare up at the light overhead.

Soon enough, Rachel comes by with my order. A bacon, egg, and cheese sandwich on an everything bagel, paired with a large coffee.

I look up at her and smile, feeling a twinge as I notice again how pretty she is, how youthful. Her healthy brown hair cascades down her shoulders, not frayed and stringy like mine. She's fresh and put together, while I'm worn out and falling apart.

Rachel still has her whole life ahead of her—I feel like I'm on the back end of mine.

I made the wrong decision about whom to marry, and now the die has already been cast. I almost feel compelled to say something to Rachel, share with her some of the wisdom I've gained a little too late, but I hold myself back.

We're friendly, but we certainly don't have the sort of relationship where I can dish out unsolicited advice about her dating life.

"Is everything okay?" she asks, mistaking my morose expression for displeasure over the food. Hastily I shake my head and manage another smile.

"Was thinking about something else, sorry. Everything looks great."

Rachel nods. "Good. I'm—I have to leave early today, so if you need anything, Hannah can help you, okay?"

"Sounds good, thank you."

Rachel is already heading back to the counter, moving with purpose. I raise the sandwich to my mouth as I watch her go. I hope she's okay. It's clear despite her ever-polite manner that something is bothering her.

The sandwich tastes excellent as usual, though it doesn't spark the joy in me that it usually does.

All of life feels dull, in fact, or possibly I'm the one that is. Removed, distant. Empty.

Having my heart stomped and crushed has left everything a little less bright than it was before. I loved the wrong man, and in this case, it was a life-altering mistake.

I hope this is just a temporary state, and not a permanent shift that has occurred.

Tears form at the corner of my eyes again, but I wipe them away speedily. I'm *not* going to break down in this cafe while eating an egg and cheese bagel. I will not.

Commotion to my left brings my head up as Rachel says goodbye to the other girl behind the counter.

To stop myself from crying, I focus hard on her as she heads toward the front door. Rachel has her coat on, buttoning it up as she starts walking to the exit.

"Be safe," Hannah calls out, causing Rachel to pause with her hand up to push against the glass door. She glances back toward the counter, and my entire body goes still. Then she's gone, but my skin continues to buzz.

It takes my sleep-deprived, despondent brain a moment to make the connection, but then it hits me.

Rachel is wearing the *exact* same coat as the girl Spencer met at the bar—and turned away from me at that angle with her hand raised, she was the spitting image of her, too.

CHAPTER 27
ABBY

y rubbery legs somehow manage to carry me toward the door, as I go after Rachel. My mind races.

It can't be possible, can it?

But as she turned and faced the counter, it was like I was looking at the photo I took of them all over again. I don't even need to check my phone—the image is burned into my brain.

Long brown hair, black puffy coat with a spotted faux fur hood, hand raised.

I race through the cafe, moving quickly and drawing the eyes of the other customers as I run through the door, which hasn't completely shut from Rachel's departure.

"Rachel," I call down the street.

My shout captures the younger woman's attention, and I get another shock when she turns around to face me.

The way the fur hood folds on Rachel's jacket is identical to the jacket in the photo, I'm sure of it.

Now I do go for my phone, unable to resist. I have to know for sure. With a trembling hand, I draw the phone from my pocket.

Rachels is standing still, looking at me with an expression

of alarm on her face, as if I might tell her the cafe is on fire and it's her fault.

"Yes?"

She's clearly more than a little confused. I tap over to my photos and pull up the image to confirm it. There it is. A perfect match.

Running my tongue over my cracked lips, I close the distance between us with my phone clasped tightly between my fingers.

"This is you, isn't it," I begin, mouth dry as I hold the phone out so she can see it.

It takes a moment for my hand to steady, and another for Rachel to see what I'm trying to show her. When she finally does, I watch her eyes go wide and hear her sharp intake of breath.

I nod eagerly. "You were on a date with a man named Spencer here, right?"

Rachel takes a half-step back, her confusion deepening as she opens her mouth but doesn't speak.

The poor girl has no idea what's happening. She probably thinks I'm stalking her, so I rush to explain.

"He's my husband—or was—or, still is, I guess. I followed him that night," I say.

Rachel glances up at my face, her eyes even wider now. She looks ready to bolt or maybe to defend herself. I try to slow my breathing a little. No doubt I look and sound volatile, and Rachel expects me to explode on her, or something.

I lick my lips again and take another breath. "That is you, right?"

I don't know where my boldness has come from. Maybe after everything that's happened, I just don't care anymore.

All I want is the truth.

Rachel swallows and gives a tiny nod confirming that yes, she is indeed the girl in the photo.

"Listen, Abby... he-he said he wasn't married. He wasn't wearing a ring. He... I—" Rachel stutters, but I raise a hand.

I'm not mad at her. She's just a young woman who went on a date and then saw that date on the news, arrested for murder.

And I have no doubt at this point that Spencer *wasn't* wearing his wedding band when he met her. I don't even care about that right now.

I'm consumed by what this new information means. A freight-train of thoughts is barreling through my skull, and the rattle is loud enough I can hardly think straight.

Where does this fit in with everything else?

Suddenly, nothing makes sense. I knew Spencer was seeing someone else, and after noticing how similar the girl found dead in the park looked to the girl in the photo, I'd assumed they were the same person.

The coat, the hair style and length—they all looked the same.

A strange new thought hits me that sends a chill running down my spine and curdles the few bites of food in my stomach.

What if Spencer met up with Rachel that night and then met up with *another* similar-looking woman, the one whose body was found the next morning?

Serial killers typically have types, don't they?

If that was the case, Rachel barely escaped the same fate as those other poor girls.

But if Spencer was with Rachel all night... he has an alibi.

To get to the truth, I'm going to have to ask for information a wife doesn't ever want to know.

I swallow and force myself to take in a quick breath.

"After the date, what happened? I mean, did you... go home with him?"

Rachel eyes me for a moment, as if trying to gauge whether I'm going to strike her.

"We... uh, went back to my place," she confirms in a small voice.

"But the news... they're saying he... Abby, I'm so sorry. I had absolutely no idea. If I had I would've never—"

"It's okay," I say. "It's not your fault. What time did he leave your place?"

Rachel looks away from me. "It was really late, probably around, maybe about four in the morning. That's why I'm so confused..."

Another thunderbolt strikes me.

That means Spencer *was* with Rachel the whole night, and he got back to our place just before sunrise.

Surprisingly, I'm not all that bothered by the fact that my husband definitively slept with another, younger woman. There is a much more pressing thought that has taken center stage.

There is no way Spencer could have killed the girl in the park.

He was with Rachel during the time the police say the second killing took place.

Rachel is speaking again, but I can hardly hear her over the roar of blood rushing in my ears.

I blink, forcing myself back to the present.

"...headed home to call my parents and ask what I should do next. I just found all this out at the cafe, and...Abby, I don't even know what to say. When I saw the news—I mean, I can't even imagine what you're feeling, but it must be even worse than I feel."

I shake my head and turn away, rocked by a sensation like the ground has been yanked out from underneath me again.

Rachel's revelation doesn't add up with the police narrative.

Behind me, she calls, "Abby? Abby, are you okay? Are you mad at me?"

I don't answer, and I don't stop. As I walk away, I whip

out my phone and rattle off a text to Katherine, telling her she needs to meet me at my apartment immediately.

I shoot past Mud Pot and the remains of my breakfast sitting abandoned inside it. The hunger I felt earlier has been completely replaced by a burst of adrenaline as I run to our apartment.

There is more to this than I originally thought.

It was literally impossible for Spencer to have killed Lexi Hardman, so how did a lock of her hair end up in my toiletry bag?

CHAPTER 28
SPENCER

The walls of the jail cell are covered in long scratches that I have a sinking feeling might be marks left behind by fingernails.

The paint is chipped and peeling, and there's a smell in here that tells me dozens upon dozens of bodies have occupied this small room prior to me.

I don't know how this could've happened.

Sure, I've made mistakes in my life, but who hasn't? It's not like adultery is a crime.

That's the worst part about being here. I'm innocent. I *didn't* kill those girls.

One minute I'm living large, successfully juggling all the women in my life, and the next moment I'm getting thrown to the ground by police officers in my own apartment as they arrest me for the murder of two women.

All I wanted was to take my wife on a cruise. A nice, relaxing, rejuvenating cruise. Is that such a crime?

I lost control again, too. It was shameful, and Abby saw it. Just like Shannon did.

My psychiatrist, Dr. DeLuca, says outbursts like that are the result of my narcissistic self being forced to confront a situation in which I don't get my way. I still highly doubt I'm a narcissist—I'm way too smart for that—but either way, I have to admit it got ugly.

Looks like I didn't have control after all. Maybe I never did.

Admittedly, it doesn't look good.

That first girl, the blonde—Liz, maybe? I was sexting with her through the dating app, but we never ended up meeting.

Still, my lawyer says the fact those braids of hair were in my home is going to be pretty hard to defend. Combined with the fact that I did have contact with her, it doesn't leave him much wiggle room.

The second girl, Lexi... something.

Her, I have no idea about. I'd never seen her in my life, apart from the horrible photos they showed me in the interrogation room. She did kinda remind me of the coffee girl I was with a couple days ago.

Rachel. Finally got her name.

I think they were even wearing the same kind of coat, which was weird. And very unfortunate. Now they think I'm a murderer.

Somebody shouts out in the corridor, the noise distant and strangely inhuman. It jars me, jerking me upright as my eyes snap back open and my heart pounds a little faster.

Every time I close them, I can't help but see the way Abby was looking at me—like she really thought I killed those people.

The hurt in her eyes. For a moment, it made me regret everything I'd done to her. It really wasn't her fault I didn't love her anymore.

"Visitor," one of the guards says with a bang of his baton on the cell door.

I sit up on the thin mattress.

It must be Abby.

I'm going to apologize to her and do my best to convince her of the truth.

Standing up, I run a hand through my hair and tug on my prison garb, smoothing it out as best I can.

It's a far cry from the tailored suit I was wearing just a day ago.

I walk along in front of the guard who's escorting me down the hallway to the visiting room. The men in the cells around me scream and shout obscenities as I pass. Some of them even spit. Animals.

We take a turn down another hall and walk toward a door that reads, *Visitation Room*. Through the window in the door, I see a row of chairs stationed in front of partitions, all with a piece of thick plexiglass separating them from the other side.

That's where Abby will sit, the two of us separated. I guess that's how it will be for the rest of our lives if I can't get out of this.

Suddenly I wish I'd been able to stay faithful to her. If I'd been able to manage it, I wouldn't be in this situation right now.

The guard wrenches the door open.

"Chair Two. You have thirty minutes," he says gruffly.

I step inside and look for chair two, finding the number in faded paint on the chair to my right.

Walking toward it, I expect to see Abby's face on the other side of the glass—but when I get there, it's not her.

It's *Jane*.

I feel an annoying twinge of disappointment in my chest but keep my face expressionless as I slide into the seat.

Actually, why do I feel sad that Abby's not here?

She isn't supporting me, and if she truly believes that I could've done something like this, why would I even want to be with her in the first place?

Jane on the other hand, she showed up for me. At least, I hope that's why she's here.

If she's here because she's figured out I lied about her being the only woman in my life, I could be in even more trouble.

Much to my relief, the pretty redhead smiles at me brightly as she picks up the phone. I do the same on my side, shifting a little in the cold plastic seat to try and get comfortable.

"Hey handsome," she says rather casually, considering my situation.

From her tone of voice, you'd think the two of us were just meeting for coffee in some cute place on the Upper West Side.

"Hi," I say.

My tone doesn't have nearly the same level of chipper. Maybe it's because I've spent the last few hours dodging human excrement flung from the other cells.

I've got no idea how this is going to play out. I guess I've already lost Abby, but I haven't lost Jane, yet. Maybe she can even help me out like she did last time.

I have to handle this right, though. My gut tells me I need to own up to the truth—or a version of it, at least. That usually works. It confuses people when you mix just enough truth with the lies.

"Listen, Jane. I—"

"You look great. I've missed you," she says, interrupting me.

She smiles, revealing those perfect teeth that always turn me on. The tightness in my stomach begins to settle. At least someone misses me.

My own wife apparently called the police on me and suspects me of killing two girls like I'm some kind of monster or something.

"Thanks," I reply.

Already I'm starting to feel a little bit better. It's amazing what a beautiful woman smiling at you can do for your spirits.

"Have you been enjoying yourself in here?" she asks.

I scoff.

Jane frowns a little, confusing me.

"Hmm. I would've thought you'd appreciate a few hours away from that wife of yours."

Any good feelings that had been building up leave my body like a wet fart. My stomach clenches as I gape back at Jane, who's looking at me pertly.

How could she know I'm still married? I never wear my ring at work or talk about Abby. I've been telling her I'm separated and almost divorced.

I guess she is here to rip into me after all.

Blinking, I'm at an uncharacteristic loss for words.

"I… we were …are… getting divorced," I toss out weakly.

It's a pitiful lie, and we both know it.

Jane doesn't seem at all flustered however, which surprises me even more.

"I love to see you squirm, you know that? It's so cute. I've known all about your wife for years—since back when you met her. I don't care about her," she says.

My eyebrows come together. "You don't?"

"Nope. Want to hear even better news?"

Jane is smirking again, but there's something off about it.

Her grin is a little too wide, a little too joyful. My heart begins to beat faster as I adjust my grip on the heavy plastic phone. Sweat has started to coat my palm, making it slick.

"Uh, okay."

"Your wife doesn't care about you now either. Not after what you've done," Jane says, wagging a finger at me.

I'm not sure if this is some sort of cruel joke or what, but it isn't funny. Jane is still smiling like she's just said the most hilarious thing in the world, and it's really starting to irk me.

Okay, so I cheated and got caught. Big deal. She came all the way down here, just to rub it in?

I shouldn't be here in the first place.

I didn't even kill those girls. Not like I expect Jane to believe me either, but still, I have to try and defend myself.

"I want you to know I didn't—"

"Hush. The evidence *is* rather overwhelming, Spencer. It would take a miracle to get you out of this. That…or another culprit."

Jane's eyes are locked on mine. I don't even know what this conversation has turned into. Her words aren't matching up with the smirk on her face, and it's making my stomach twist even more.

"What do you mean?" I ask slowly.

"I'm the one who's always loved you, Spencer, not *her*. She believes you did this, but I *know* you didn't. I'm the one on your side, not her. It's always been me, you understand that?"

I blink again, unsure of what to say. I guess it's technically true that I've known Jane longer than I've known Abby, since I started working with her a year before Abby and I met.

But Jane and I didn't even become a thing until a few months ago, so I'm not sure where all this is coming from.

"In fact, I started working at Bateman & Co because of you, Spencer. I just *adore* seeing you in a suit," Jane says with another brilliant smile.

Her gorgeous face is so mesmerizing I'm having trouble separating the vision from the slightly disturbing words coming out of her mouth.

Is she honestly saying the only reason she took the job at Bateman was to be near me? We've worked together a long time. That would mean this whole time, all these years…

My lips open, but I can't really come up with anything to say. There's only confusion, and a small inkling of something in my gut that grows with each new sentence that passes her full, glossy lips.

Dread. I'm feeling dread.

"Abby agrees with me on that—the suit thing, I mean," Jane says with a nod, her eyes shifting away from me.

"Probably the one thing me and that useless halfwit can agree on."

My heart slams against my ribs, hard enough to make me actually wince as a cold sweat breaks out across my brow.

Jane has met my wife.

"What…" I begin but trail off as my eyes meet Jane's again.

All of this is so strange, and so sudden. She's acting totally differently than she does with me at work.

With a start, I realize that's what is throwing me off so much about her smile. It's manic… triumphant. Like she's just pulled off the world's greatest magic trick, and she alone knows the secret of how it was done.

"What… what's going on?" is all I can muster.

Jane tilts her head coquettishly but doesn't answer my question.

"I've got to run now, but I'll see you soon, okay? Love you."

She says it so casually, like we'll run into each other at the supermarket or something later this week. As if I'm not being held under suspicion of double-homicide.

"Jane?" I say, gripping tight to the phone with a clammy hand.

The things she said have left me feeling odd. There's something I'm missing here, something I'm not quite getting.

Jane is not the person I thought she was—so who is she?

She's already set her phone receiver back on the hook. She reaches up to the slab of heavy glass between us and presses her palm against it, skin flattening enough that the color blanches from her skin, and I can see the grooves of her fingerprints.

A guard enters her side of the room. The sound is muffled with the heavy barrier separating us, but I can still make out the man as he speaks.

"All set Ms. May?"

My brow furrows as surprise strikes me, rocking me back in the hard plastic chair.

Ms. May?

Jane's last name is Walter, not May. But where have I heard that last name before?

Then it hits me.

Understanding dawns right as Jane flashes me one last parting smile and gives me a little spread-finger wiggle wave.

All I can do is stare after her as the truth spreads through my bones like a fast-acting toxin. I grip the phone so hard I nearly crack it.

Jane Walter and my wife's best friend Katherine May are the *same person*.

CHAPTER 29
ABBY

Where is Katherine?

She's taking forever to get back here, and I need to talk over my new discovery with her. Nothing is adding up.

I pull out my phone to shoot her another text but pause as I realize I've already sent four in a row without an answer from her. It's obvious that I'm looking for her, and if she could, she would've already responded.

Another message isn't going to help anything except for my anxiety, and then only for a few seconds. I pace back and forth in my living room, which is still in a state of utter disarray after all the chaos of yesterday.

With the time I've got until Katherine arrives, I decide to gather my thoughts as best I can and lay out the facts so I'll be able to present my case to her in a sensible way.

Taking a deep breath, I settle onto one of the kitchen bar stools and lower my forehead to the marble.

It's cool to the touch and helps to calm my racing mind.

Fact one—Spencer couldn't have killed Lexi Hardman because he was with Rachel at her place.

Fact two—that means that someone had to have planted Lexi's braid in our apartment, but why?

It doesn't make any sense to me. If I had happened to come across it accidentally, it wouldn't have meant anything to me, unless I knew that Spencer had been out the night before with a girl who bore a resemblance to Lexi Hardman.

My mind begins to spin out as I try to put the puzzle pieces together and form a complete picture. Only it's not a flat jigsaw puzzle but a three-dimensional one. And my sleep-deprived brain isn't exactly at its best.

I need Katherine here to help me dissect this thing. I glance over at my phone, but the screen is still dark.

Where could she be?

With the assumption that Spencer didn't kill Lexi still rolling around my mind, I think back to Elizabeth Waters, the first girl who was found in Central Park. Detective Sullivan said there was no evidence that she and Spencer had ever met up, and that was backed up by the messages between the two of them.

We figured that was just shoddy police work, that they must have had a rendezvous at some point—but what if it was actually the truth?

That Spencer hadn't met up with Elizabeth, and so he *didn't kill her either*.

I lick my lips as my heart pounds faster. The police could have been right all along. And if they were, there is a single question that still needs to be answered, and fast.

How did two braids of hair belonging to dead women wind up in my bag?

I can't come up with any plausible explanation. Could he have had an accomplice or something?

Spencer lured the women and set them up for the kill, and his partner did the actual dirty work? It just all seems impossible.

There's absolute anarchy in my chest as feelings froth

around inside it like waves in a storm. Guilt, anger, confusion. All of it mixing together in my mind as I think of Spencer and his handsome face—then the desperation in his eyes as he was carted out of here in handcuffs.

Though I know now what a good liar he is, his frantic denial felt like the truth.

A knock at the door snaps my head up. I'm ripped from my thoughts and left sitting on the barstool blinking.

"Abby?" comes a muffled voice.

Thank goodness. Katherine is finally here.

A second longer spent in my own mind, and I just might begin to lose it. I push off the marble countertop and scurry around the side of the island to unlock the door and open it for her.

Katherine looks up as the door swings open, flashing me a smile with her perfect teeth. It's the first time I've seen her with her hair down. She's wearing cute matching gloves and a scarf–so put together.

When she smiles at me, it feels like everything is going to be okay.

She's here now, and we can figure this thing out together.

Relief washes over me as the words I've had on spin cycle all day begin to pour out.

"Spencer didn't do it—didn't kill the girls, I mean. At least, I think. I mean he couldn't have acted alone. I don't know, I—"

Katherine holds up a hand and scoots past me. "Woah, woah. There's a lot there."

I gulp down a breath and nod quickly. I must look half-insane to her.

To be honest, I feel it.

The emotional rollercoaster I've been on over the course of the last few days has left me nearly senseless and definitely strung out.

"Let me use the bathroom first, and then we'll dive into

whatever, okay? I should have gone before I left work. Now I'm desperate," Katherine says.

I nod again as she makes her way into the bathroom. The door claps shut, leaving me alone in the too-bright kitchen again as my thoughts rocket through my brain.

A dull buzz interrupts me before I can spiral again. I whip my head around, looking for the source of the noise, and realize the buzzing is coming from my phone on the countertop.

It's upside down, moving ever-so-slightly as the phone trembles with the force of the phone call.

I scoop it up but don't recognize the number displayed on the screen. The toilet's muffled flush reaches my ears from the bathroom as I decide whether or not to pick up.

After another second of hesitation, I swipe to accept the call and hold the phone up to my ear.

A robotic voice greets me, informing me it's a call from an inmate at some correctional facility in the city. Then there's a recording of Spencer saying his name. The automated voice returns. "Do you wish to accept?"

A pang of emotion slashes across my chest at the sound of Spencer's voice. The way he said his name sounded strange, as if he were stressed or panicked when he recorded it.

Maybe I shouldn't, but I reply that yes, I agree to accept the call.

I can hear the sink running in the other room as I wait a few moments for the line to connect.

Finally it does, and Spencer begins talking instantly, his words running in a steady stream before I can even say hello.

"Abbyyouneedtolistentome, okay? Katherine is not who... I don't know who she is but watch out. I think she might've had something to do with the murders."

My entire body locks up, and the hairs on my arms and the back of my neck lift. I can't hear the water running in the bathroom anymore.

"Abby?" Spencer asks, but I don't respond to him.

I'm too busy responding to the chill running down my back. Turning around slowly, I let the phone slip away from my ear, as the puzzle pieces finally begin to click into place.

Katherine is leaning against the bedroom doorway, and the look on her face is utterly terrifying.

CHAPTER 30
ABBY

"That's Spencer, isn't it?" Katherine asks in a biting tone.

I clutch the phone, still hearing my husband's tinny, panicked voice coming from the other end.

"What's going on?" I ask, my throat constricting.

This is more than just a friend being mad at me for being foolish enough to accept a collect call from my cheating, incarcerated ex.

"It *is* Spencer, isn't it. I can't believe it," Katherine says, a snarl curling her features, her gaze locked on the phone in my hand.

"Hang it up—now."

When I don't obey quickly enough, she takes a step forward and snatches the phone out of my stunned hand, hitting the end-call button with her thumb.

Then she flings it to the side, where it lands out of sight with a crunch.

She looks almost upset, but not quite. It's an odd look I can't quite place.

"See, I would've thought some time in lockup would've shown him the truth, but I guess not," Katherine says.

She's still taking slow steps toward me, while I'm backing up. Her entire demeanor seems different from any other time I've seen her. It's like a whole different person came out of the bathroom.

"I don't understand," I say in a small voice.

Katherine's odd tone is scaring me. Spencer's call scared me. Suddenly, I don't like that it's just me and her in my apartment. The walls have me trapped inside.

Katherine tilts her head and sneers. "You think I actually *enjoyed* being your friend? I only tolerated you to learn more about Spencer."

Her lip curls back as she jabs a thumb into her chest.

"He loves *me*, not you. Me. He just... doesn't seem to understand that, even after everything."

I keep backing away, nearly tripping over my own feet to get away from her.

My back comes up against the wall, my skull thudding into the drywall. I've got nowhere left to go.

Katherine's words swirl around in my head, only serving to confuse me even more.

She loves Spencer, too?

But she's never met him. In all the time I've known her and been married to Spencer, I've never once been able to get them in the same room. A jolt of electricity runs through me as realization dawns.

I realize now that was on purpose.

"Have you... have you been seeing Spencer behind my back?" I manage, my voice squeaking out.

Katherine gives a barking laugh. "Seeing him? Baby, I've been doing a whole lot more than that. And for longer than you two have even known each other. He belongs to me, not you."

My heart pounds in my chest as Katherine takes another step toward me.

I don't know what's going to happen if she reaches me, but I'm scared to find out.

There's a scary tension in the air, like a lit stick of dynamite.

It feels like Katherine is going to explode at any minute.

The only thing keeping her together is that smirk that is slipping more and more the more aggravated she gets.

"If only Spencer would get that through his thick skull. I couldn't believe it when he married *you* of all people."

Her words cut through me like a whip. Tears burn my eyes, even though I cannot afford to break down right now.

Her tone is just so hateful, so full of spite.

The way she ridicules me with her eyes, as if she couldn't see why Spencer would ever want to be with someone like me.

"Please stop," I say, as the tears begin to fall.

"I'm his soulmate. I'm the one who was there for him, especially after his first wife's disappearance," Katherine hisses with another thumb-jab at her chest.

"Where were you? Probably frolicking around with someone else. Not loving Spencer, that's for sure," she adds.

"That's not true," I try to shout, but the words eek out as little more than a hoarse whisper.

Katherine is close enough now that I can smell the perfume she's wearing. It's sickeningly sweet, and not something I've ever smelled on her before.

I recoil against the wall, turning a cheek as if that will somehow shield me.

"Spencer never loved you. That's got to be obvious by now, even to a brainless, halfwit woman like you."

There must be at least a tiny spark left inside me because I come back with, "He apparently doesn't love you either, since he's been sexting and sleeping with half the women in the city."

Katherine lets out an offended huff but recovers herself quickly.

She laughs and shrugs her shoulders in a gesture that's meant to be nonchalant but is a little too quick and jerky.

"He's been sowing some oats, getting it out of his system so he'll be ready to settle down once he's rid of you. And I'd say he's learned his lesson about spreading himself too thin, haven't you?"

She purses her lips into a little pout. "I feel bad, leaving him alone in such a scary place. He won't be there much longer, though."

I blink, and for a moment the fear fades away as I try to grasp what she's saying.

"See, no one knows it yet, but there's another pretty girl lying dead in the Park," Katherine says, "and weirdly enough, she's got *your* DNA on her."

A ringing fills my ears as I sag against the wall. I feel like I've been punched. Just like she did to Spencer, Katherine is going to frame me for the murders.

"With Spencer locked up, he couldn't possibly have done it," she says. "Soon enough, they'll complete their investigation and realize Spencer never met Elizabeth or Lexi, either. So... that really leaves only one other way those braids could've gotten into your apartment."

That bone-chilling smile returns.

"The braids were found in *your* toiletry bag, after all. And won't the police be delighted when they find the murder weapon hidden in the bathroom too," she finishes.

My head shakes as my entire body trembles. Katherine nods her head.

"Can't you see the headlines? Vengeful wife kills off husband's playthings, then blames the cheating hubby for her crimes? I'd buy that."

A cold sweat breaks out across my face. She's planned it

all out perfectly. Why wouldn't the police believe what she says?

She planted the murder weapon somewhere in the bathroom and somehow planted my DNA on another victim's body. I don't know if there's any reason they'd doubt her.

Katherine licks her lips as she takes another threatening step toward me. I slide to the side and move in a slow half-circle, my back coming up against the kitchen island as she continues to prowl after me.

"You know, your blind loyalty to Spencer is almost admirable. The anonymous note I sent would've been enough to get most women suspicious of their husband instantly, but you clung onto your faith for *ages*," she hisses.

Katherine lets out another short laugh. "Basically had to drag you through every step. Between you and the police, I was afraid my plan wasn't going to work after all."

"You're insane," I shout, lunging for the couch to put some space between us.

My former friend lets out a barking laugh. "No, Abby. I'm in love."

She reaches into her back pocket for something, but I can't tell what it is.

A gun?

I have nowhere to hide. My entire body tenses as her arm comes back around. But it's not a gun she's holding. It's a phone.

"What are you going to do?" I ask, my words coming out strangled as sweat pours down my underarms.

Katherine's eyebrows pull together, and she smirks.

"What do you mean? You just admitted everything to me. I have to call the police, it's my civic duty."

"No—please," I beg her. "Don't do this,"

But it's no use. She's determined to destroy my life.

Katherine holds eye contact with me as she raises the device slowly to her ear. I can hear the phone ringing.

"Don't. Katherine, don't," I plead.

She chews her lip, seeming to debate something.

"Maybe you're right. Should I just kill you? Maybe that would be easier. Can't risk you somehow convincing the police of your side of the story."

I swallow hard, feeling my body begin to tremble.

"You do have a certain… innocent look to you," Katherine finishes in a snippy tone.

Her head cocks to the side. I can see a strange glitter in her eyes that sends waves of panic through me.

My palms are soaked in sweat, my entire body trembling as the phone in her hand continues to ring.

Katherine's thumb hovers over the end-call button. Meanwhile, her other hand reaches behind her again.

This time, she pulls out a switchblade.

She holds the two objects out to either side of her as if they're balancing weights on a scale.

"Life is full of tough choices, isn't it?" she says.

"Tell me, Abby, *as a friend*… what would you do in my position?"

CHAPTER 31
SPENCER

I don't know what to think anymore.

Sure, it's great to be out of jail, but now the police are telling me that it was *Abby* who killed those girls. Apparently she admitted everything to Katherine—or Jane, whatever her real name is—and then took off before the police could get there.

At first, I refused to believe it. There's simply no way that woman is capable of anything like that. If she was, I think I would've been a lot more wary of cheating on her.

No, throughout all my time having known her, I've never even seen her yell at somebody, much less hurt someone.

Then again, there's allegedly some pretty conclusive DNA evidence.

And I know she really does love me.

The cops speculated she killed those girls in a jealous rage after she learned I'd been flirting with them online.

I don't know what to think about that. Or why she would kill another one while I was locked up. They found the third victim just hours ago, her cold body lying under a bush in Central Park.

To think I called to try and warn her about Jane. Crazy.

She might've been in the act of hiding the body even while I called her. That's probably why she hung up on me.

But then I think about Jane—or Katherine—whatever, and how odd our conversation was when she came to visit me in jail.

Her behavior there still has me worried. And the fact she's been going by two names and masquerading as my wife's friend... well, it's not exactly normal.

So as the police cruiser drops me off in front of my building with a hasty apology, I'm left staring up at my apartment with a tenseness in my body that makes me feel strange.

Worried, maybe? Weird.

I'm not used to feeling this way, and I'm not sure whether I'm worried about my wife—or about myself.

Apparently no one has seen Abby since she slipped out after telling Jane everything. She must've used the back exit where they store the trash bins, otherwise the cameras in the lobby would've picked her up.

There's a manhunt on for her, big enough that it's made the news.

I shove past a few reporters who have taken up positions on the sidewalk in front of our building. It only takes them a second to recognize me, and then I'm being pestered with questions as I pick up the pace toward the revolving door.

All of them jostle for position in their quest to interview me, but a neighbor coming out of the building shouts to make way so he can leave.

I'm grateful for that, as it allows me to slip into the lobby and take a breath. What a whirlwind the past few days have been.

I'm back in my suit from the weekend, having been allowed to change into my clothes again once they dropped the charges and released me from custody.

I'm sure I smell *fantastic*.

What I need now is a long shower and a cold beer. Then maybe I'll try and piece all this together.

There's a lot to think about, what with Jane's declaration of love and Abby's apparent murderous jealousy.

Another pang of guilt hits my chest as I punch the elevator button. If I hadn't been fooling around on her, she wouldn't have killed those girls. The only reason they died is because they knew me—or looked like someone who did.

Guilt is another feeling I'm not too pleased with. I just need to get drunk and try to forget all of this craziness.

I step into the elevator, finding my blind neighbor Mrs. Glenn in there already.

The old broad is so blind and deaf she probably has no idea I'm even in here with her.

"Who is that?" she asks.

I'm not looking to make conversation, but I don't want to be rude.

"Spencer Stevens, Mrs. Glenn," I reply.

"Who?"

This time, I decide to stay silent. If she realizes it's me, she'll probably try and invite me over like she's been trying to do since I moved in here. I made the mistake of going over once, right before I met Abby. I couldn't get out of that musty room fast enough.

Better for Abby to be the one who has to deal with her, not me. Though I guess now grocery duty might fall on me. I let out a sigh as a light tune plays in the background of the elevator.

Despite how insane everything is, somehow I know I'll come out okay. I always do. In a weird way, it's almost a mirror of my experience after Shannon disappeared. The suspicions, the reporters, the frenzy.

It died down eventually. I bet this will, too. It always does.

I let out a breath, allowing my pulse to slow a little.

Yeah, I decide.

Within six months, no one will even remember any of this.

I'll be able to start meeting other women again—maybe even find a new wife.

The elevator doors pull apart on my floor, and I step out into the hallway in front of Mrs. Glenn.

It feels a little surreal walking back to my door, back to my comfortable apartment and all its fancy things after the squalor of the jail cell.

After having spent the last day or so in lockup, it's nice to be home. I can't wait to kick my feet up and drain a few IPAs.

I think there's a game on tonight, too. That'll help take my mind off things. Shower first, though.

I turn the key in the lock, and the door swings open.

Inside, the apartment looks pristine. My brow furrows. It was in a state of utter disrepair when they dragged me out of here.

What, did Abby clean up the place in between murders, just before fleeing?

Whoever did it, at least I don't have to. I head over the fridge, finding that it's been stocked with food, too.

Abby even got my favorite brand of beer.

She must have gone shopping before all this went down.

Things really do always work out for me.

I grab one of the beers and pop the cap, taking a deep drink as I unbutton my shirt.

A creak behind me whirls me around.

I come face-to-face with a woman stepping out of the bedroom.

It isn't Abby. It's *Jane*.

She's got a towel wrapped around her body and another around her hair. Her skin is pink from just being in the shower.

"Welcome home," she says with a wide smile.

"How did you get in here?" I ask, my grip tightening around the beer bottle.

After our last conversation, I'm not sure I want to be spending any more time around her. Seems like all the women in my life are a little unstable.

Jane laughs like I've just asked the silliest question in the world.

"I have a key, silly."

She scoops it up off the counter. My heart beats a little faster as my eyes latch onto the keyring it's attached to. It's Abby's.

I know because hers has this little white fluffy heart on a chain. And now there it is, dangling from Jane's hand.

"Was wondering when they'd let you out," Jane says in a flirtatious tone.

I set down my beer bottle, eyes darting around the room. Jane makes her way to the couch and flops down like she owns it.

Her bare feet come up to rest on the glass coffee table as she leans her head back and rolls it toward me.

"What's wrong?"

I lick my lips, not entirely sure how to proceed. I was not expecting *anyone* to be here when I got home—not Abby, and certainly not Jane.

"I just… uh, I don't really know how to feel about this," I say.

Hopefully that came out right. While I can't say for certain, it feels like there's a strange energy that Jane has around her, almost violent. I don't know how I missed it before.

Her face clouds, and she sits up straighter on the couch.

"You *still* don't understand, do you?" she asks in a sharp voice that cuts through the air like a knife.

The sound is jarring and makes me stiffen.

"Understand… what, exactly?" I ask.

I'm beginning to think it was a mistake sleeping with Jane to begin with.

Maybe this is why they say not to fish off the company dock.

"That I did all of this for *you*. So that we could finally be together," Jane says.

Her eyes bore into me.

"All of this…" I begin, and then it clicks.

Jane leaps off the couch and takes an excited stride toward me. Her face is bright as her eyes dance across my face.

"Now you get it. Finally, you get it. I was beginning to think I fell in love with the wrong man," she says. "I like *smart* men."

I take a step back, and then another. My shirt back comes up against the cool metal of the fridge as my heart pounds. Abby didn't kill those girls.

Jane did.

She flashes another smile as she leans against the kitchen island.

"You see? Abby had to take the blame. She'd been in the way for far too long. In the way *of us*."

Her tone suddenly brightens. "Look, I made drinks."

Jane points to the countertop, where a couple of Cosmopolitan cocktails sit.

"What have you done?" I ask, my voice quivering slightly.

"What I had to," Jane replies with a shrug.

"But that's the best part—now we have a clean slate. Abby will be blamed for all the murders. We can be together now," she adds.

"Jane… where is Abby?" I ask, my throat closing in.

Jane cocks her head. It makes her look even more deranged.

"What do you care? Didn't you hear me? *We* can be together now. No more hiding or sneaking around or waiting for never-ending divorce proceedings. I took care of that."

Another pang hits my chest. Has Jane done something to Abby?

My old work-fling is just standing there, looking at me with one of Abby's hair towels wrapped around her head. She's an absolutely stunning woman, but I'm beginning to understand her beauty is like a peacock's feathers—distraction.

I swallow hard, working to choose my next words very, very carefully now that I know what she is capable of.

"Jane, what did you do to her?" I ask slowly.

She tongues a molar, looking as if she's deciding what to tell me. The seconds pass, counted off by the pounding of my pulse inside my head.

Finally she throws up her hands with a roll of her eyes.

"Ugh. Nothing, okay? Nothing. I let her run off—looks more convincing of her guilt if she's on the run."

A wave of relief washes over me, and I sag against the countertop beside me. I don't know if my conscience could handle another death on my behalf.

"But who cares? She's gone, and the longer she's gone, the guiltier she looks. Even if she does get caught eventually, no one will believe a word she says," Jane says. "She takes the blame for all the murders..."

She pokes a polished fingernail into my chest in rhythm with her staccato words. "And. You. Are. Free—because of me. Because I forgive you for all your little dalliances—which are now in the past by the way."

A strange light switches on in Jane's eyes as a new idea hits her.

"You know," she begins excitedly, "I bet we could even tell the police she had something to do with the disappearance of your first wife–finally free you from that as well."

Now it's my turn to be confused.

"I didn't do anything to Shannon," I say.

Jane rolls her eyes dismissively. "Right, right. Sorry babe, I know it's a sore subject. That's why I want to pin it on her."

My arms cross in front of me as a sudden defiance fills my

body. I shake my head, straightening from my slouched position.

"No, Jane, you don't get it. I really *didn't* touch Shannon. I have absolutely no idea what happened to her."

Jane looks completely taken aback.

"To be honest, after you came to the prison, I was beginning to think *you* did something to her," I say.

"But… you had me lie to the police for you," Jane says in a quiet voice.

My head is shaking back and forth again.

"Well, yeah, I had to. Me having unaccounted time looked bad. But I wasn't doing something to Shannon. I was with another woman."

That's why I couldn't tell you the truth.

Anger and confusion flash across Jane's face in equal measure as the truth finally comes out. I push past my discomfort and shake my head again.

"I'm telling you the truth. I didn't have a thing to do with my first wife's disappearance."

Jane looks like she's been slapped.

"So you really *didn't* kill her," she says, her words a whisper.

"No," I say slowly. "Did you?"

She shakes her head as I stare at her.

I know I didn't kill her, and now it's been confirmed Jane didn't either—*so who did?*

CHAPTER 32
SHANNON
SEVEN YEARS AGO

There isn't much time.

He'll be home soon.

I take a final glance around the bedroom. Our bedroom.

How happy I once was here. Young and in love. Those memories exist now only in the framed pictures lining the dresser.

Shaking myself, I zip up my duffel bag. There isn't much at all in it, but I don't care. It'll have to be enough. I just need to get away—while I still can.

The car is packed for our trip, ready and waiting for my husband to come home.

When he does, he'll find me already gone.

I don't know what will happen after that, but I don't care anymore.

All that matters is getting away.

I take a final glance around the room before heaving my duffel bag strap up onto my shoulder and stepping through the doorway.

The living room is quiet, with only a couple of lamps illuminating the space. More pictures. More memories.

Good riddance.

The journey down to the parking garage takes longer than I want. It seems like the elevator stops on every floor, people stepping on and off.

Seemingly every resident in the building has somewhere to go today. Never before have I been jealous of those living in first-floor apartments.

Each time the door opens, I imagine him standing there on the other side, his chin lifting, those bright blue eyes coming up to pin me against the wall.

I make it to the parking garage and look for our car. I wouldn't even have come down here, save for the fact that he packed both our passports.

Something tells me that was on purpose.

The car's parked around the corner. I hurry across the cement floor, my footsteps sounding extra loud to my ears as they echo through the cavernous space.

As I go, I pull out the braid in my hair, just to give my anxious hands something to focus on.

I'm alone down here, as far as I can tell. Even still, my pulse has reached jackhammer levels. I have to be quick about this.

Get the passport, get out.

When I round the corner, however, I stop walking.

There's our car—and right beside it, the suitcase.

Only the last time I saw it, it was in the trunk. My heart pounds against my ribs. How did—

A scrape from behind me. I jerk around.

It turns out I'm not alone in the parking garage after all.

To my surprise, it isn't Spencer that emerges from the shadows.

It's some... *woman.*

She's blonde, like me. She's pretty, too.

I stare at her with wide eyes, questions blasting through my mind.

Did *she* take the suitcase out of our car?

Why would she do such a thing?

"Who—" I begin, but my voice falters as I catch sight of her expression.

Since emerging from the shadows, she hasn't stopped walking toward me. Even now, the distance continues to close. And at her pace, she doesn't look like she's about to stop.

I stumble backwards, toward the car.

The blue suitcase is a few feet from me.

"Going on a trip, were you?" the woman asks sharply.

Her voice seems to echo through the garage. She's just a couple feet from me now, her mouth set in a hard line. I blink several times, trying to regain my equilibrium.

With as scrambled and nervous as I was already feeling and how strange this interaction has started off, it takes me a moment to comprehend the question.

"I... no, I'm not," I say finally.

The woman smirks.

"I knew you'd lie. You're just like I imagined you were, Shannon."

As the woman says my name, everything changes.

Goosebumps rise across my skin, and my chest tightens. I take a few more steps backwards, but the woman moves toward me again.

How does she know my name? I've never seen her before in my life.

Stumbling into the suitcase, I realize something else. Her hair isn't just blonde like mine—she's wearing it braided the way I usually do mine. As I meet her eyes, I realize she's even done her eyeshadow like mine, and her eyeliner, with little wings at the outer edges.

A ball forms in my throat.

"Who are you?" I ask in a small voice, my grip around my duffel bag handles tightening.

"His next wife," she says coldly.

My chest pounds as I realize I have nothing to defend myself with. All I'm carrying is my phone, wallet, and a few sets of clothes.

"You're not going to go anywhere with him—ever again," the woman says.

I shake my head, but I'm so freaked out I can hardly speak. "No, I–I, listen…"

The last thing I see is the vibrant red of a crowbar flashing through the air.

CHAPTER 33
ABBY

I would do anything for love.

That's something I've always prided myself on—that sense of total devotion and a willingness to do whatever it takes, to go all the way.

Sometimes, there are obstacles. That's okay.

The way I frame it? Obstacles are just tests of your devotion. If it's truly strong, there's nothing you can't overcome.

Shannon, simply put, was an obstacle.

From the moment I laid eyes on Spencer Stevens, I knew he was the one for me. I saw him exiting his building one day, looking so ravishing in that navy suit.

He worked in Midtown at the time.

I had to know more about him, this man I'd fallen in love with at first sight on the street.

It hit me like a bolt of lightning, and I just knew.

Spencer was going to marry me.

After following him home however, I discovered one issue. Spencer was already married to *Shannon*.

But as I watched them from the apartment I rented across the street, I saw that Spencer did not love her. There were little things, like how he wouldn't kiss her goodnight for very long, or how they never seemed to linger in each other's presence.

Little messages he was sending out to me, letting me know that he wasn't happy in his relationship with his wife.

I understood his messages perfectly. He wanted out. He wanted me.

I wanted him right back, and so I began to plan.

One day, while watching through the window, I saw he'd gifted her a blue suitcase. It was massive, gaudy and loud. Loud enough that I understood the message.

Spencer wanted Shannon to go away.

And just like that, the idea struck. A way to make her disappear.

It was simple. Easy, really. Wait for her in the dark in the garage, wearing all black.

I knew which car was theirs. In a city like New York, it's easy to blend in, easy to go unnoticed as you watch and learn.

I learned that it's easy to just walk right into a parking garage—if you're nicely dressed and act like you belong.

I learned where their parking spot was. I learned what time Spencer left his office to walk home from work at night and how long it took him to get there.

Shannon headed for the SUV, and I came out of the shadows. Now *she* would learn what happens when you stand in the way of destiny.

It was over in minutes. I worked quickly, and didn't waste any time on conversation. Besides, I already knew everything I needed to know about her.

After taking her down, I emptied the suitcase Spencer had bought.

Wouldn't you know it—she fit inside perfectly.

It took another couple minutes to mop up the blood with a few pieces of Shannon's resort wear, but I got it done. All of those went into the suitcase with her, along with her wallet, phone and passport.

Walking home afterward, I cried. Even though I knew I'd done it for a good reason, that didn't make it necessarily *feel* good.

I cried again when Spencer came home, and the police cruisers showed up.

They looked over the apartment and the building as a whole as I watched from across the street, waiting anxiously for a glimpse of Spencer.

Finally he appeared next to the window, and I remembered why I'd done it—for true love.

Then he was taken in for questioning, which had me in tears all over again. They couldn't possibly pin this on him, could they? He hadn't done a thing to that woman.

I picked a time when I knew for sure he'd be at work. I turned off Shannon's phone and remembered to grab her passport so it would appear that she simply ran away.

It took longer than I expected, but finally he was released.

From there, the rest of the story played out exactly how I planned it in my head. Random run-ins at the coffee shop on the corner, flirty glances.

My special laugh where I throw my head back and allow guys a look at my chest while pretending I don't notice them staring.

Soon enough, Spencer was mine.

We loved each other. At least, I thought we did. Then to find out he was cheating on me... for a moment, honestly, I thought everything was lost, and that we didn't have true love after all. That I'd married the wrong man.

As I watch through the spyhole in Mrs. Glenn's apartment next door, however, I can finally breathe easier.

Spencer didn't kill those girls, and he didn't work together with Jane to conspire against me, as she tried to make me believe.

The conversation I'm watching between the two of them

confirms it—he looks terrified of her, as he should be. She's a monster, and she needs to go.

I shift my position and press my right eye up to the hole I drilled through the wall a long time ago.

It's tiny and sits just below the lip of a hanging shelf in a way that makes it almost imperceptible unless you're specifically looking for it.

Once I realized Spencer was Mrs. Glenn's neighbor, I knew I had to befriend her. It was easier than I thought. She has no children and no other family, after all.

Before Spencer asked me to move in with him, I used to come over and just watch him. I could spend hours simply observing him going through his day at home.

Drinking coffee, getting dressed, all of it. I just love him so much, I can't possibly get enough of him.

I haven't used this peephole since we got married, until now. Until Jane tried to cut me out of the picture, tried to take Spencer away from me.

I was never going to run. The only thing I wasn't sure about was whether Spencer was in league with Jane this whole time.

I'm so, so pleased to see he wasn't.

He is who I thought he was, and that is such a relief.

He was concerned about me.

When he asked what Jane had done to me, I could see the concern on his face. I could hear it in his voice, and I fell in love with him all over again.

I've seen what I needed to see. Pulling my eye away from the peephole, I roll my cramped shoulders and take a deep breath.

I just needed to confirm that Spencer still loved me, like I knew he did.

A warm feeling washes over my body as I take a step back, smiling. Beaming really. I'm back in love again. No more of this tortuous state of not-knowing.

The fact that he was with other women doesn't bother me now, as I know I'm the one he truly cares about. I saw it written all over his face when we'd turn on the news—he felt nothing for those girls. They were just objects to him, not people he loved, cared for.

Not like me.

Mrs. Glenn's spare bedroom is pretty barren. Like I said, I don't spend too much time here anymore. Besides my sleeping bag on the floor, there isn't much else.

Well, besides the reach-in refrigerator housing the blue suitcase, of course.

It hums along quietly beside me as I glance over at it. Mrs. Glenn really is an angel for letting us use this room for storage.

It reminds me of a different time, when Spencer and I weren't together. All of Jane's talk about the recording of me dragging the suitcase reminded me of that time too. I just hate thinking about it. I was lonely and unloved then.

My eyes drift over to the opposite wall, where the words I painted years ago still sit.

I LOVE YOU, SPENCER. The memories of the hours I spent painting that phrase all around me, over and over and over again. It took days to wrap the entire apartment in my love. Every surface—the bathroom tile, the kitchen cabinets, the ceiling. Good thing Mrs. Glenn is blind.

All of it is a testament to us. To my husband. I hear the front door click open, and then the gentle wheezing of Mrs. Glenn fills the air around me. I've been careful to stay quiet, though she is remarkably hard of hearing. Once I'm sure she's settled into her chair, I slink out of the bedroom and walk over to the kitchen to pull open a drawer.

Mrs. Glenn doesn't react in the slightest.

I turn back around and look over the contents of the drawer.

There are so many different ways to deal with Jane inside

it. My stomach tightens as I think about Spencer witnessing this part of me.

It's the side I've always kept hidden, the uglier part that I didn't want him to see. Raising my head up, I realize something. Spencer loves me, all of me. That's what marriage is—unconditional acceptance.

I *want* him to see and accept this part of me now, to strengthen our relationship.

To tighten our bond.

I've always known I was meant to be with Spencer. Sure, he's imperfect, but aren't we all?

I love him all the more for it.

CHAPTER 34
SPENCER

The apartment door swings open, nearly giving me a heart attack.

I blink hard, thinking for a moment I'm hallucinating or something.

But no, that's really Abby standing there in the doorway.

"What are *you* doing here?" Jane snarls from behind me.

Abby takes a step inside and closes the door. She looks pretty good, considering she's supposed to be on the run for murder. I wonder where she's been staying that has a shower and a change of clothes in her size.

My wife holds eye contact with me, ignoring Jane altogether.

"Just wanted to confirm it," she says.

Jane's eyes flash. "Confirm what?"

Abby, still looking only at me, beams. "That Spencer loves me, not you. Not anyone else, just me. Now I know."

My heart pounds so loudly I wonder if the other two can hear it. Abby takes another step toward me, and I know she's expecting me to do something. Somehow I manage a smile, though not without a hundred questions surging through my head.

I'm also wondering what she's doing back here after Jane gave her the chance to run.

The way Abby is acting, it's like she's been listening to the conversation Jane and I were having. Like she's been watching us. A cold sweat starts up again at my hairline as I shift back and forth on my feet.

"No, he does love me," Jane hisses.

Her head whips over to me, pinning me with a glare. "Right Spencer?"

Abby stands beside me, looking directly at me. I have to do something, have to say something. Swallowing hard, I shake my head.

"I don't," I say to Jane.

It's true and always has been.

To be completely honest, I don't think I love Abby, either. Especially not if she did something to Shannon.

What have I done to deserve two women this crazy?

Abby beams again as Jane sags. It feels like all the power in the room is moving to this side, where my wife stands. She turns to me, her braided hair lying prettily on her shoulders.

"I'm so sorry for doubting you, babe," she says before pulling my face down to hers and kissing me.

The kiss is passionate, fierce. I'm ashamed to say that despite everything, I can't help but feel some movement below the belt. Abby pulls away as Jane lets out a pained howl from the other side of the room. She rushes forward, a massive switchblade in her hand.

I've no idea where it's come from, as she's wearing nothing but a couple bath towels.

"Woah," I shout, scrambling backwards.

Abby, however, doesn't move. Instead, she reaches into her jacket and pulls out a handgun.

My jaw practically hits the floor. Jane jerks to a stop, the knife frozen in mid-air as her eyes catch on the weapon as well.

"Where did you get that?" I ask, fighting to get the words past the boulder that's formed in my throat.

I didn't know Abby even knew how to hold a gun, let alone owned one.

She smirks as she raises the gun higher, pointing it directly at Jane.

"I guess we all have our secrets, don't we, babe?"

I drop my head and look down at my chest as heat fills my cheeks. It's all I can do to hope that Abby doesn't shoot me next, after what I've done.

Jane lets her blade clatter to the floor, licking her lips nervously. The malice that was so plain across her face moments before is gone now, replaced with a terrified look that seems out of place on such beautiful features.

"Okay, you win," she says in a rush.

She takes a few steps back, her feet tripping on the edge of the carpet as she backpedals. Abby moves forward, still holding out the gun.

"I know," Abby replies simply and cocks the weapon.

This is not good. I huddle down in a squat, attempting to disappear. This is all so insane. Pressed up against the kitchen cabinets like I am, one of the handles digs into my back.

Regardless, I don't dare come out of hiding. My eyes are squeezed tightly shut. I don't even want to breathe too loudly.

I'm afraid if I make one wrong move, say one wrong word, Abby is going to lose it and do something to me.

I think I might've really messed up, might have pushed her past her limits.

I can't see what's going on in the living room, as the cabinet obscures my view. There's talking in low voices, and then a wet *thud* followed by a strangled cry.

Another heavy squelch that makes me wince. My heart leaps up into my throat.

My hands are trembling. I had no idea my wife was capable of any of this.

"Hey Spencer," Abby calls airily from the living room.

My heart sinks. She hasn't forgotten about me. Licking my lips, I rise to my feet.

My footsteps around the kitchen counter and into the living room are slow and cautious. I don't know what I expect to find. She might blow a hole in me as soon as I come into sight.

I keep my eyes trained on my feet—at least until I see the first splotch of blood that stains the rug. The apartment is dim, only a single lamp lighting the space.

Lifting my head, I see Abby standing tall beside the couch, and Jane huddled in the corner. Jane has her hands pressed against her mouth, where a busted lip gushes blood. White specks that I realize with a jolt are teeth speckle the ground in front of her.

I freeze, not sure if it's anything worse than missing teeth. The weak lighting obscures the violence like a veil.

Abby glances back over her shoulder at me and smiles. There are flecks of blood spattered across her chest and chin. My heart careens against my sternum.

I'm terrified of this person in front of me. I'm utterly and completely terrified of my wife.

"P-please," Jane says through a mouthful of blood, "I-I let you go, didn't I? Gave you a chance to run."

My eyes shift over to Abby to see what she's going to do. She has all the power here. With a jolt of alarm, I find that she's looking back at me again.

"What do you think, babe?" she asks.

My voice catches in my throat. I can't look at Jane whimpering in the corner, at the bloody mess that her face has become. There's no way I can focus on anything but Abby. Her eye contact has me absolutely pinned.

"I..." I begin but trail off.

Does she seriously want me to decide whether Jane lives or dies?

This can't be happening—it's all so insane, I can hardly believe it's real. But it seems I'm actually standing here in my living room, watching my wife hold my mistress at gunpoint.

No words come. I glance back and forth between the two women, wishing with everything inside me I could be anywhere else right now. Even that rancid jail cell would be better than this.

That old sensation begins to build in me at the realization I'm no longer in control. I'm starting to feel like a cornered animal. Pretty soon I might start acting like one.

It's almost like Abby can sense it because she gives me a hard look.

"No more tantrums sweetheart. They're unattractive."

The wild energy within me withers and dies like a hurricane dissipating over land. I won't be able to weep and thrash my way out of this one.

Abby blinks, her large doe eyes impaling me.

"You do *love* me... don't you?"

Vaguely I recognize it's the same question I posed to her just days ago.

I nod hurriedly. I don't know what would happen to me if I said no, and I don't ever want to find out.

"Good," Abby purrs.

She turns back to Jane, who lets out another fearful whimper.

"Then we need to decide what to do with her, babe. Together."

EPILOGUE

ABBY

I know everyone says it, but I truly am the luckiest girl in the world.

Letting out a yawn, I roll over and breathe in the scent of Spencer's body beside me in the bed. He's still sacked out, lying completely still. It's better than him snoring, that's for sure.

He never does that anymore.

The sheets feel so warm, making me reluctant to get up at all. I know I have to, though. Despite everything, life still goes on. I've got work today, so that means I've got to start getting ready.

I lift my head to see Spencer's face and find that he's awake after all. He's staring up at the ceiling, unblinking.

"Morning," I say through a yawn.

He jumps a little, seeming surprised that I've spoken. His eyes flick down to me, wide for a moment before resettling.

"Good morning," he croaks.

I love the way his voice sounds in the morning. So deep and gravelly. I raise up to one elbow then scale his chest until I'm at the right height to plant a kiss on his lips.

Closing my eyes, I sink into the kiss and feel the warmth of our love wash over me. Spencer's lips quiver only a moment before relaxing.

Then I'm up and heading for the bathroom, looking a mess but happy to be here.

After washing up, I make my way into the kitchen and start on the eggs. Spencer joins me a few minutes later, his movement stiff.

"Sleep okay?" I ask over one shoulder as I get the eggs into a bowl for whisking.

He nods quickly. "Fine."

Part of me thinks he's not being entirely truthful, as the dark bags under his eyes this morning seem even heavier than they have the past couple days. Clearly, something is disturbing his beauty sleep.

I'm not sure what, as I haven't slept better in years.

Things worked out perfectly, just as I planned.

After some initial confusion, the two of us were able to convince the police that Jane was the one behind the Central Park murders, not me or Spencer. My recording of their conversation certainly helped.

Of course the detectives wondered why exactly I had a listening device in my own apartment. I told them I'm really into home security, and that seemed to satisfy them.

They had a confession on tape after all. That, coupled with both my testimony and Spencer's, as well as Rachel's statement and the knife used to slit the throats of all three victims, and the case was closed.

No more girls had turned up dead. New York could stop worrying about the Central Park Slayer and move on to the next sensational headline.

Authorities suspect Jane/Katherine fled the state, possibly even the country. I believe Detective Sullivan used the phrase *disappeared into thin air*.

She hasn't used any of her credit cards or pulled any money from the bank. She does have a history of using aliases, so they say she's likely traveling under yet another assumed name.

We've promised to let them know if we ever hear from her again.

They shouldn't hold their breath.

My spatula pushes the eggs around the pan as Spencer sits stiffly at the kitchen counter. He looks absolutely exhausted, but I won't mention it. I'm just glad everything worked out, and that he loves me.

Really, that's all that matters. Once I've got the eggs cooked, I reach over and lift the fresh pot of coffee that is whistling hot.

"Want some?" I ask.

Spencer gives a small shake of his head.

"Aw," I say, "but I made it just for you, babe."

He swallows, his eyes flicking up quickly to my face.

Then he nods and raises his mug from its position beside his plate. "Then yes, I'll have some."

There's just a tiny tremor in his hand as he holds up the mug.

I smile and pour the coffee, relishing this glorious morning, the two of us sharing our special little just-us time before the day gets hectic.

This is the way life should be, all the time. The way it's meant to be.

While Spencer eats, I return to the bathroom to apply some makeup. Going to the vanity. I pull open my drawer to get my makeup bag, and my eyes drop to my secret place where I had once stored proof of Spencer's infidelity.

I've forgiven him, as I believe in letting bygones be bygones. He's only human, after all.

Besides, I have more concrete proof now, anyway.

Proof that is tucked away next door, in Mrs. Glenn's spare bedroom with the two reach-in fridges that now occupy most of the space. It's getting quite crowded in there. A smile touches my face as I think about the suitcases inside them.

One is blue, and very expensive. The second is red, like Katherine's hair.

I smile to myself again as I apply mascara. My life really is perfect. And everything really does work out for the best.

Like every married couple, Spencer and I have been through a lot together. The things we've been through recently, while challenging, only made us stronger.

We're closer now than we've ever been before.

Spencer has been nothing but incredibly nice and caring to me lately, and I'm sure there will be no more dating apps or coffee girls from now on.

I think it's because he *finally* understands just how much I love him. We truly are meant to be together forever.

As I've always said, I just can't get enough of him.

Though if I were ever to find out that he loved anyone else, well… I'd be worried for him.

There's a chance he might disappear—just like his first wife.

Thank you so much for reading *His First Wife*. I hope you enjoyed it. If you'd like to read my FREE psychological thriller novella, *The Weekend Trip*, sign up for my newsletter by heading to jackdanebooks.com As a member of my mailing list, you'll be the first to know whenever I have a new book release and get behind the scenes information on my stories and my writing life.

If you had a great reading experience with this novel, would you mind taking a minute to post a review on

Amazon? A few words is all it takes, and it will truly make a difference in my career as an author. Reviews are so important in helping other readers find great books that are worth their valuable time and attention.

Thanks so much for reading :)

Jack

ALSO BY JACK DANE

THE APARTMENT ACROSS THE HALL

ABOUT THE AUTHOR

Jack Dane writes thrillers and psychological fiction that largely takes place in New York City, where he lives. When not writing, Jack enjoys going to jazz clubs, taking people-watching walks in the Park, and exploring the city by night, where he picks up ideas for his next book.

Get a FREE copy of his thriller novella *The Weekend Trip* by heading to jackdanebooks.com

You can connect with Jack on Facebook by searching Jack Dane Author!

Copyright © 2025 by Jack Dane

All rights reserved.

No part of this book may be reproduced in any form or by any electronic or mechanical means, including information storage and retrieval systems, without written permission from the author, except for the use of brief quotations in a book review as allowed by U.S. Copyright law.

All books written by Jack Dane are written entirely by him. No AI is used in the creation of Jack Dane's books.

This book is a work of fiction. Names, Characters, places, and plot are either products of the author's imagination or used fictitiously. Any resemblance to any person, living or dead, or any places, business establishments, events or occurrences, are purely coincidental.

For rights inquiries, please contact the author directly at jackdane@jackdanebooks.com